# THE WARDEN WATCH

## From the Annals of Myrtle and the Blood-King

By AR Horvath

1.

Published by

# ATHANATOS
## PUBLISHING GROUP

# THE WARDEN WATCH

## From the Annals of Myrtle and the Blood-King

By AR Horvath

1.

Published by

## ATHANATOS
### PUBLISHING GROUP

# THE WARDEN-WATCH

ISBN 978-1-936830-73-2

For more information on future installments from the *Annals of Myrtle and the Blood-King*, visit: www.thebloodking.com.

AR Horvath is also the author of the Birth Pangs series. Learn more at www.birthpangs.com.

# How You Can Help The Author

The reader may not realize it, but the way books are made, bought, and sold, has changed quite a bit. In the old days, books were bought in bookstores. Today, they are bought over the Internet. In an earlier time, people heard about books in newspapers and magazines. That still happens, of course, but now people hear about books in many other ways, such as through social media. In some ways, that is good for authors. They do not have to pay a lot of money to get heard. There are challenges though: *everyone* is trying to get heard! With all that 'noise,' it can be hard for the authors you enjoy to get noticed.

That's where you come in.

If you enjoy what you are about to read, and want to read more by the author, you can help. How? Tell *everyone* you know about the book. That is a great start.

To learn more about how you can spread the word about this book, be sure to check out the section at the end where more ideas are given.

I hope you enjoy *The Warden-Watch*, the first in *The Annals of Myrtle and the Blood-King*.

Sincerely,
AR Horvath

# Chapter 1

It was about mid-afternoon, and the sun had already dropped quite a bit from its noon-day position at the top of the sky. A telephone pole cast its long shadow over the tool shed. The first thing that caught my attention was the sound of something ceramic getting tossed to the ground, presumably on account of the wind. Something wasn't right. The trees were waving in the wind and the swing on the swing set was creaking, but there wasn't breeze enough to push pottery around. I turned around to see what was broken and, out of the corner of my eyes, I saw a shadow leap, as though startled.

The strangeness of this observation did not register in my mind.

I continued to gaze blankly in that direction until it dawned on me that there were now two long, narrow shadows lying across the tool shed: one explained by the telephone pole and the other explained by... Well, that was the thing. There wasn't an explanation for this second, new shadow. There was no corresponding object like there was with the telephone pole.

Still, as odd as that might be, I wasn't feeling particularly inquisitive. I probably would have never thought any more about it except that as I sat there on the back deck, the new shadow began rotating in a circle, like the hands of a clock. I could remain no longer in my summer daze; I scratched my head. The shadows of the trees were sweeping back and forth on the lawn as would normally be expected. *That* is proper behavior for a shadow.

No sooner did it occur to me that here was something worth fighting the heat and humidity to investigate did the insolent shadow cease moving. It was as though it had spied me spying it, and froze. It was all to the worse, however, since now the shadow was perpendicular to the shadow of the telephone pole! Not only was there a shadow with no corresponding object, but it was lying in the completely wrong direction.

With a sigh and a groan, I stood up. Some instinct kicked up in me, and I felt like if I was going to make a move to learn more, I had better be sly: this shadow was clever. I nonchalantly made my way in the direction of the shed. The shadow didn't move. The wind was still blowing, the trees were swaying and the swing set was creaking, but the shadow held fast.

I knew that when I got closer I wouldn't be able to see on top of the shed, so I decided to make off for the tree-line, which was about halfway up a modest hill. Then, when I circled back, I'd be on the slope of the hill and would be able to see the roof of the shed for a little longer. I feigned that I saw a butterfly and wandered towards the trees. I had never tried to outwit a wayward shadow before, but I hoped it didn't take much more cunning than this. After all, I am just twelve years old. I have only begun to fill up my bag of tricks.

Though my legs took me on a long, out of the way ramble, I never took my eye off of the top of the shed. It was probably for this reason that the shadow refused to budge. Even as I changed my perspective as I circled the shed, I couldn't deduce what was making the shadow. The more I thought about it, the more I was certain that I had seen that shadow leap into existence out of nothing. I steeled myself; one doesn't let one's guard down around such renegade shadows!

As I finally drew near to the shed, it seemed to me that the shadow was now moving, but just a bit. It was very hard to tell. Could it be that the shadow knew I was approaching, and it thought that by slow, incremental movements, it could fool me? Do shadows have brains? I concluded that my best bet was a surprise burst of speed to take the shadow off its guard. That is what I did.

When I got closer to the shed, I leapt towards an old milk crate, alighted upon it, and pulled myself up so that I could just get my eyes over the edge of the roof and could see on top of the shed. Who was surprised more?

Take a piece of paper and hold it so you are looking at its edge. If you knew nothing else about paper, you would think it was just a thin, white line. Now take the paper and slowly tilt it. The surface of the paper gets bigger and bigger until at last you can read clearly what is on it. My first glimpse of the shadow was a bit like that. As I made my leap, the shadow 'tilted' to reveal a larger form. Only, what I saw was not a drawing or a scribble. It was a full bodied ape-man, poised to jump, and hiding in plain sight on top of my shed!

When my eyes locked with its eyes, it fell over backwards, startled. I was pretty startled myself, and I fell off of the milk crate. The ape-man had fallen off the shed on the side opposite of me and I, like a fool, gathered up my five-foot, three-inch self and darted around to catch it in the act of retreat.

It was Big Foot. Sasquatch. The North American Yeti. It was a huge beast and I was a little man, but I just had to get one more look!

It was tall and hairy but its face was wise and startled, rubbing its head in apparent pain. When I came around the corner of the shed and looked upon it, it regained its composure and made like it was going to run away.

I don't really know what I was thinking. Maybe I felt that if such a large thing was scurrying away in fear from me, then I had nothing to fear from it. Maybe I knew what all the adults would think if I told them what had happened but had nothing to show for it. More truly, I considered the fame I'd enjoy if I came away from the incident with a fistful of hair that couldn't be identified. At any rate, before it could make its run to the woods, I was already leaping towards it. I grabbed hold of its arm... its eyes grew large and white... and my eyes grew large and white... as what I was doing started to settle in.

It jumped!—I was still attached!

To my astonishment, the world grew larger and larger. Big Foot and I were getting smaller and smaller as we hurtled through the air. I just barely had time to notice that we were falling into a cleaned out mason jar that had been resting against the edge of the shed for who knows how long, before even the jar was so large it seemed like it contained the sky... and then it was dark, dark, dark.

"And that," I said, "is how I came to be in the Great Cavern Council of the Wardens."

I was explaining myself to an assembly of large, hairy creatures. I was standing in the middle of a circle of their elders. The one whom I had clutched was sitting in the circle, too, but he was as far away from me as he could get. He had his head buried in his hands and was rocking back and forth in apparent shame. I had learned that these tall and stringy beings described themselves, strictly speaking, as 'Mammalites,' but preferred to be called Gate Wardens, or just Wardens. In any case, though, I think they were giving me rough translations for my benefit. One thing I learned was pretty unnerving: the Great Cavern which I was currently standing in apparently existed *below* the mason jar that was laying outside our shed, and if these... people? were to be believed, the Great Cavern was actually below a speck of dirt that was below a pebble that was below the mason jar.

And that is hard to get one's mind around, whether you are twelve, twenty, or sixty-three.

# Chapter 2

Having given an account of how I came to be among them, the council of elder Wardens now regarded me with an impassive silence that went on and on, such that I finally couldn't keep my attention on my predicament. My mind wandered, and then my eyes. I tried to catch a glimpse of my captors, but the layout prevented it. A bright light from an unknown source flooded the center of the cavern, illuminating myself and the weeping one. However, outside the light, it was a tarry black. Numerous columns rose up around me in a circle. They were equally spaced, with just their faces catching the light, and the bulk of their substance concealed in the dark. I only knew that the Mammalite elders were present because they too would sometimes lean forward, and their features would transition from nothing, to shadow, to form, before they melted back into the formless void. No doubt they were each sitting in a throne and occasionally adjusted themselves. It was only because of this that I had confidence that they resembled the one who still avoided all contact at the other end of the chamber.

"You put us in an impossible situation, Son of Adam," a voice emanated from the far end of the Grand Cavern. I didn't know what to say to that, so I said nothing.

Another voice spoke: "For thousands of years the Wardens have been hidden from the sight of your race, and only because of this do we Wardens continue to survive. If you were to depart from us, untold harm could come to us."

"Yet, he cannot stay!" declared another.

"An impossible situation," repeated the first voice.

I ventured to speak, "I promise to say nothing of what I have seen! No one would believe me anyway!"

This was met with silence.

"He must be put to death," said the one who insisted I couldn't stay.

"He has done nothing to warrant that sentence," the first voice rejoined. I thought that there was a hard edge to it.

"And what about *him*?" the vindictive one asked, apparently referring to the one who still cowered far away from me.

5

The second one now spoke again, "He also has done nothing to warrant punishment."

"Agreed," said the first voice.

"An impossible situation!" declared the third voice. Upon the final syllable, the voices of the assembly began making a noise, like a hum with rhythm: "Uh-Hummah-Hum-Hum-Hummah." It was low, and gravely, and seemed to represent agreement by the assembly with what had just been spoken. I found the sound frightening, however. It echoed throughout the chamber and beat me from all sides and permeated deep within me, so that I could even feel my heart vibrate with it. My own heart agreed with the assembly, quite against its will.

"They shall redeem themselves for the harm that they shall inflict in the future," the first voice announced. He continued, "We are caught between competing moral principles and woe to us if we compromise either of them. There will, most assuredly, be untold harm to follow from this turn of events. We must endure them, suffer them, and cry out for mercy. Only let us endure these unknown calamities through no fault of our own and not because we justly deserve them."

The third voice protested, "Have we not already endured so much through no fault of our own? For thousands of years we have been caught between 'competing moral principles.' For thousands of years we have endured calamities on account of the Fall of Adam. Will there not come a day when we act only in the interests of the Wardens?"

There was a round of humming, but not as many as before.

The first voice spoke: "It has been decided, and not another word shall be spoken."

"Uh-Hummah-Hum-Hum-Hummah," they all said.

To my surprise, the owner of the first voice now stepped into the light, and I was able to inspect his features in detail. My first impression was that he looked much like Chewbacca the Wookie from the Star Wars movies, but the second impression obliterated the first. The speaker's facial features were much more human than I expected. The fur was indistinguishable from clothing. It was clearly part of his being, and yet at the same time it was fashioned like an accessory: there were clearly delineated lines between arms and chest, and waist and torso. The last thing I noticed was that much of the hair I saw came from his head and not from his body, as I had initially supposed. It stretched back from the cheeks and middle of the forehead and flowed in waves along his body, right down to his feet. I was struck with the realization that I was here standing before a king, and so instinctively I fell to my knees, with my head down.

The second speaker spoke: "It is well decided."

I looked up, and I saw now that all of the elders had stepped into the light, and, to my deep astonishment, were all kneeling before me!

I stood up in horror, "I am only a boy!"

The assembly laughed, its laughing a variant of the same low, rumbling hums, as before. I noted that there was one Warden that was on its knees, but was not happy to be so. The other heads were bowed, but this one cast a steely gaze at my direction. The Wardens now stood. There wasn't any one of them that wasn't less than twice my height.

"You do not yet know why we kneel," said the King.

The King turned his attention to the young Warden that had remained cowering throughout the entire ordeal. The King strode over to him and placed his hand on his shoulder, and said, "Arise, Marmor, son of Gleckor, son of Haledash, son of Shim, son of Brecken, son of Kandish, son of Soledad, son of Mitmah, son of Felang, son of Halter, son of Mammal."

Marmor arose.

"Your duty and task from now until relieved is to instruct the Son of Adam in the ways of the Wardens to the extent that is permitted. Carry out the duties appointed to us in general and to you in particular, with him as your companion. At the time that seems right, we shall send him back to his own, and at that time endure what follows."

Marmor cast a glance at me. I now saw that he too had the regal air that the King possessed. Here in the cavern he seemed much less like the wild beast he had appeared to be outside my shed.

Marmor spoke, "Father, I shall do as you instruct."

Marmor's father, the one I regarded as the King, turned his

eyes upon me and inquired, "And what is your name, Son of Man."

"My name is Casey," I stammered.

"That is not your name," the King replied, "but it will do for now."

"I should know my own name," I unwisely protested.

"I walked with your father in the cool of the day at the dawn of time and again in the shadowlands. Your name without his name is not your name. Someday you will know your name in full, but it is not for me to tell it. For now, we shall indeed call you 'Casey,' and that will be enough."

# Chapter 3

The King and the council of elders disappeared from the cavern, leaving Marmor and I alone to regard each other. I never saw any of the elders leave, hidden as they were in the black canopy of the cavern's shadows. The King, however, threw a glance at me over his shoulder before stepping into the pitch black. He nodded as if to acknowledge my predicament, and then melted away.

For the first time, I realized that I was far away from my home and would be so for possibly a long, long time. I felt a pang on my insides as I thought about my mother, my father, my brothers, and my sisters. I thought about my bed: how to this point I had despised it, crammed between dressers and bunk beds on account of the fact I had to share my room with my brothers! But now I would take that bed a thousand times over without hesitation, for that bed meant safety, certainty, and security, under the protection of my vigilant parents.

I dabbed away a tear. I didn't want Marmor to see my tears and think that I could be pushed around. This way of thinking was all rot, of course, and I knew it almost immediately. After Marmor and I had been left alone in our thoughts for a few minutes, he pulled himself up to his full height and strode over to me—his long, gangly legs making the number of strides just three. He extended his hand to me, and I took it. He helped me to my feet. With a little gesture that meant 'follow me,' he turned and stepped into the black that enveloped the cavern.

I hesitated for a moment as I watched him utterly disappear from sight. What was I stepping into? What would happen? How would I find my way when I could not see my hands in front of my face? Realizing there was nothing else to do, I shrugged, and stepped. I kept stepping, my hands outstretched in front of me. I faintly heard the soft pad-pad of Marmor's footsteps ahead of me, so I groped in that direction.

This went on for quite a long time. Never did my hands touch anything before, beside or behind me. For all I knew, I was marching off into the expanse of a starless sky. There were no boundaries, no walls. There were no echoes. There was only the gentle footfall of Marmor ahead of me.

I was long past the point of desperation when finally a bit of light began to show. It now seemed as though I was in a tunnel. Then there was the proverbial light at the end of the tunnel. The further we went, the more Marmor's silhouette was thrown into contrast against the light. Not long after the light had first appeared, it had become a brilliant and blazing light, blinding me such that once again I felt compelled to protect my going with one hand in front of me—the other was shielding my eyes. "Marmor!" I called out in fear, as the light brought with it heat, almost unbearable.

The instant I called out, though, the piercing light dissipated completely, and I found myself falling haplessly onto a grassy green field, surrounded on all sides by towering trees. You may imagine the experience as being like what happens when you are going down a flight of stairs and you think that you have one more step to go, but, in fact, you have reached the bottom. Your step is the same as any other step, but your expectation causes you to stumble. It was like that.

I was so happy to be able to see normally, free from the extremes of white and black, that I laid down on my back and watched the clouds float serenely by. I smelled the scent of plants and flowers on the breeze and imagined to myself that it had all been a dream, a dream I had had while lying in the open meadow, and now I was awake.

But I saw Marmor sitting nearby, looking intently at me, and I knew that the dream persisted.

Marmor spoke.

"To think that we are here because I was startled by a falling watering can, and you happened to be there to see it!" Marmor declared, shaking his head in disbelief.

I defended myself, "It was my own house! Where else should I have been?"

"I'm just saying that the odds were so low. And that you happened to fix upon the narrow line of my body? I despair that I have brought disgrace and danger upon my people, but I cannot but think that these things were all ordained," Marmor stated.

"I don't see how I am any danger to anyone," I protested. "I'm just a boy. I only learned what the word 'ordained' means last month."

"It is something that is impossible to explain to you as yet," Marmor said patiently.

"Well, I don't appreciate being treated like a scourge just because I happened to catch a shadow!" I fumed. 'Scourge' was another word I had recently learned.

Marmor laughed, "Forgive me, Casey. I will not belabor it."

I relented.

"Why are we here?" I inquired.

"This is my appointed time and place, and I couldn't think of any reason not to appear here as duty demands," Marmor replied.

"What is your duty?" I pressed.

"You realize that these are the deep things—secrets of the foundations of the world, entrusted in particular to the Wardens, and not meant for human inspection?" Marmor cast a quizzical gaze at me.

Impatiently, I retorted, "I think we are well past 'not meant for human inspection.'"

"Alright, then," Marmor said, defeated. "My duty here is to do what the Wardens always have done, and that is to hold open the gates at the appointed time and the appointed place."

"The gates?" I asked him.

"The gates."

"What gates?"

Marmor didn't answer, but rather stood and walked about twenty feet away. He pointed at an empty space about eight feet off the ground and said, "I know that you can't see this with your human eyes, but there is, indeed, and in fact, a gate here. It is my job to throw my back against the curvature of space and time and allow them passage."

"Them?" I asked, ignoring for the moment all this business about space, time, and curvatures.

"Them. Your race has names for them such as 'angels' or 'messengers,' or even 'ghosts' and 'demons,'" Marmor explained.

"My parents don't believe in ghosts," I said matter-of-factly.

"As well they shouldn't," Marmor replied, "but demons—those angels who are in open rebellion—that is another matter."

I wanted to know more, but when I opened my mouth to ask more questions, Marmor silenced me with a movement of his hand. Then, as though listening for an oncoming train or stampede of buffalo, he inclined his ear against the sky. Then, in a marvelous instant, Marmor disappeared from my sight. I had the sensation of heat, and then, remembering that Marmor and the Wardens had some kind of ability to draw their bodies as narrow as the point of a pencil, I screwed up my eyes to examine the area where Marmor had last been.

"Aha! I see you!" I cried out triumphantly. Knowing what to look for was very helpful.

After a moment, Marmor reappeared. He seemed exhausted, as though he had just exerted himself in some endeavor. He gave me a look and said, "Our time together will not be constructive if you are not ever able to see what it is I am doing. I shall ask Father for help."

I gasped. It struck me with full-force what was being offered. I, of all people who have ever existed and ever will, was going to be permitted to see the angels of God entering and exiting our world! I had truly stumbled upon something remarkable. I was speechless; my mouth opened and closed over and over again… but I had no words.

# Chapter 4

Marmor kept the gate open all that afternoon, all that evening, and all that night. I woke up in the morning to find Marmor sitting across from me. There can be no question that any person coming across such a thing would identify it as Big Foot. I knew right then and there, if I hadn't known already, that here was the source of all those legends recorded in books and discussed on the History Channel. It was no wonder that Big Foot had never been found. It was no wonder that a dead body had never turned up. It was no wonder that their dwelling place had never been stumbled upon. They were big, all right, but they could make themselves super thin and bend light and hold open the gates of heaven, and then shrink themselves right into a speck of sand beneath a mason jar. I had to ask.

"Are you Big Foot?"

"We have been so called."

I whooped in excitement, "Do you know how amazed people are going to be when I tell them that I found Big Foot? That I know what they do, and where they live?"

But Marmor didn't share my excitement. He looked down at the grass.

"What is it, Marmor? Why are you sad?" I asked.

"Someday you will return to your people, and you will tell them our secrets. Then, your people will hunt us. There was a day when we laughed in the many woods of the earth, carrying out our work without fear or concern. But always your people came, clear-cutting the trees, scarring the plains. If it weren't for the fact that we could get small, I have no doubt we'd all be dead and gone already," Marmor explained.

"We wouldn't do that!" I cried out.

"No? I have seen it with my own eyes," Marmor stated.

I watched *National Geographic* on television, so I knew that there was some truth to what he was saying. Still, it seemed to me that humans had wised up, so I protested, "I bet for a good hundred years or more we've taken better care of the things we've discovered."

"I have watched for two hundred years, and I've seen nothing to suggest such a thing."

"Two hundred years? You're two hundred years old? Come on!" I said, incredulous.

"It's true."

"But I thought you were young, like me! That's the impression that I got," I said, scratching my head. Two hundred years seemed an awful long time to be alive, but what did I know about the life spans of sasquatches?

"I am young like you. I am quite young. In fact, I am the youngest of the Wardens, as no others have been born after me. My father is one thousand years old, but he would only be regarded as being in his mid-thirties in human terms."

"That is crazy!" I said.

I thought it out. Marmor would have been witness to many great events in human history in his two hundred years of life. He would have seen great inventions and accomplishments but also great horrors. And his father, if he was a thousand years old! What of him? The American Revolution. The discovery of America itself! What else?

I wanted to ask if the Wardens did their work throughout the world, but I was suddenly struck with another thought, which shoved its way forward in priority for expression.

"What about… other mysteries? Was there an Atlantis? An Abominable Snowman? A Mothman? What about…." But I noticed that Marmor was just shaking his head. "What, Marmor, what?"

"You humans and your curiosity," is all he said.

"You won't tell me?"

Marmor sat silently.

It was here that I realized a great truth about the Wardens: they don't lie. If they can't give an answer that is truthful, they won't say a word. I knew that this might be a good way to learn truths they didn't otherwise want to reveal. If I asked if there was an abominable snowman, and Marmor refused to answer, it probably means there is an Abominable Snowman! I put this insight into my bag of tricks.

"Someone wants to come through the gate," Marmor announced. He raised himself up to his full, massive height, and lumbered over to where he had taken position the day before. In a wink, Marmor became a thin, dark line. There was that sensation of heat again. I thought, this time, that maybe the area around him was getting a little brighter. To my surprise, Marmor quickly returned to me.

"We have got to go," Marmor said urgently.

"What? Why?" I asked him, confused.

"This messenger was for us, telling us to make straight away for the home lair."

"Did he say why?" I wanted to know.

"Does he have to? Does our obedience hinge on our understanding of the command? I do not know why, and I didn't ask. He told us to go, so we must go, and *now*," Marmor said, a little too roughly, I thought.

"Ok, OK. Lead the way," I surrendered.

"Of course," Marmor agreed.

Marmor took hold of my arm and guided me towards the edge of the woods. When we got there, keeping one of his long hairy hands on me, he placed the other on a massive oak tree, and in an instant I had the experience as in the first time we descended to the lower regions. We got smaller and smaller, and as we did we fell towards the base of the tree. Near the bottom there was a small crevice that loomed larger and larger, and it became clear that we were heading for it. As though brushing aside a veil, we went from experiencing the bright of day to the pitch dark of the inside of the tree trunk at an infinitesimal scale.

After a few more moments, we were again walking in the light. We appeared to be outside again, but I did not recognize anything. I wondered if this was what the outside looked like if you were a speck. Was I a speck? Maybe so, but that made the furniture speckish, too, and my immediate surroundings gave every appearance of an abode—though one without a roof. Marmor strode by me and greeted another Warden, "Hello, Mother," he said.

The female Wardens looked much as you might expect: humanoid, but tall and spindly and covered in hair. Like the male Wardens, her hair was not a bit scraggly. It was very well groomed. Like with the others, it was hard to be sure that the hair was not in fact a garment.

"Marmor. A pleasure. And Casey! Another pleasure!" Marmor's mother said. I should have known that the entire community knew of me.

"We were summoned, Mother," Marmor explained, drawing her attention back to him.

"Of course. Your father will be arriving—"

His father arrived. He strode onto the dais with a nod towards me, but his attention fixed on Marmor. I had thought that the Warden-king had been Marmor's father, but now I saw that I was wrong. This was a different Warden-Watcher.

"Son."

"Father."

"Wife."

"Husband."

"Casey."

"Sir?" I ventured hesitantly. What was I supposed to say? I don't know.

Just then, the real Warden-king walked into the light of Marmor's home. His arrival was preceded by a gust of fresh air, and his bearing was regal.

"You do not have much time," the King said to me. "However, you are at a great disadvantage if you cannot see what we can see. So, per Marmor's intercession—" and here, he put his big hands on my eyes—"See!" I looked around, noticing nothing different. The King continued, "Now, go! The family of Casey is in grave danger!"

# Chapter 5

Having glimpsed the domesticated life of the Wardens, I had almost reconciled myself to living among them for time out of mind. The mention of my family, and the message of danger, and the sudden knowledge that I would see them again soon, birthed inside me a pang of homesickness so severe there was actual, physical pain. Marmor did not leave me to endure my suffering for long. He was quick in his obedience, I'll give him that.

With an abrupt yank, he grabbed me and pulled me into a corridor. Unlike the previous corridors we had journeyed through, this one was awash in light. The walls were made of crystal, or something very much like it. As in the Grand Cavern, the source of the light was a mystery. Marmor was pulling me along very fast, which made it hard for me to inspect them, but I began to make out numerous etchings on the walls. I realized that the difficulty in looking at them was not merely the speed in which I blew past them. Instead, my eyes found it difficult to focus on them, because the walls were so translucent that to look at them would be like fixing your attention on a spot of air. The walls and etchings on them were so much like the light itself that I had to fight to focus on them. Whenever I succeeded, though, I saw that the etchings flashed with all the colors of the spectrum. To my surprise, I began to recognize that the etchings were pictures, apparent memorializations of events in *human* history. But this confused me, because with only a few exceptions, most of the events were humdrum scenes: a kitchen, an office, a den, a library, a bar.

"Do you recognize where you are, Casey?" Marmor asked as he pulled me along.

"How could I? This is the first time I've been here!" I replied.

"Indeed, it is not. This is the way that we took on the way to the gate," he corrected me.

"No, I don't think so, my friend. That was black, and dark, and I couldn't see a thing!"

"But that was because you couldn't See. You have been given Sight, and so now you See as we Wardens See."

This was a remarkable revelation, and I didn't know what to

make of it. I asked the obvious question, "What are all these images that I see etched into the wall?"

"We make memorials to remember great moments in history when the efforts of the Wardens have not been carried out in vain," Marmor explained.

"But I see very few battles, or wars, or council chambers, or court rooms…"

"But you see a great many conversations between friends, or interactions between teachers and students, or pastor and parishioner, or adults and children. Or, you see moments when a corner has been made in someone's thinking, and it went on to make all the difference!"

"The difference how?" I inquired.

"You may get a glimpse soon enough!" Marmor cried out. "We are here!"

The crystal corridor terminated in a wide opening. Light that was not the Light of the Wardens could be seen streaming into the opening. As I came right to the end of the corridor, I instantly recognized what it was on the outside of it: my very own homestead. This other light was the light of the sun that I knew and loved and previously took for granted. Seeing my way clearly this time, I was able to step down into my yard without tumbling head over heels.

Marmor was already ahead of me. I was shocked to see him standing next to my parents. They were standing in the small garden plot, busily weeding. Adding surprise to my shock, they didn't notice Marmor near them or even me running up to them, shouting my greetings.

"They cannot hear you or see you, Casey," Marmor said, a hint of sadness in his voice.

"I don't understand," I said. Then, there was a pang of grief like the homesickness earlier, but worse: abandonment. "Don't they miss me? Don't they notice that I'm gone?"

"But you are not gone. Look, there you are!"

And sure enough, there I was! 'I,' or a spitting image of 'I,' was wandering aimlessly around the shed, obviously bored. With a start, I remembered the scene. "But that was two days ago! Have I gone back in time?"

"Not at all," Marmor corrected. "With Him, all moments are present. There is no past, there is no future. There is only one long train of 'present moments.' On this level of reality, we experience time differently. It is hard to explain to someone who cannot step in and out of present moments at will. We do not even have time to try. They are upon us!"

There was just a small moment in my mind where I wished to point out what seemed obvious to me: if we can step in and out of present moments, then there is all the time in the world to give me an explanation. His urgency and haste put the objection out of my mind, however. He rushed to the tree line and beckoned me to follow quickly, which I did.

"Look! *See!*" he said, pointing at the empty air just before the forest took over.

I *could* see, faintly, cracks of light in the air, opening and closing. The air seemed to shiver and shake and quake, with ripples of undulating atmosphere and photons spreading out into oblivion, like a rock landing in the middle of a pond. It was odd. It was even beautiful. But then there was fear, because sometimes out of the tiny cracks a foul wind would issue forth, and it did more than make my nose turn up; it rattled me to the core.

Marmor threw his back against the splintering air. "Help me!" he cried out.

Not knowing exactly how to help, I decided imitation was my only guide. I turned around and threw my body backwards as though against a wall, knowing all along that there was no wall, only empty space, and that I would once again find myself rolling on the ground. A Mammalite joke, no doubt. Their way of initiating the new guy. But the 'wall' held. 'Odd' remains the best word to describe it.

No sooner did my back land against the fissuring sky, I felt it pulsating behind me as though something was desperately trying to get through a door. My taste of the foul wind before cemented within my consciousness the view that whatever was trying to get through was a murderous scoundrel, and I exerted all my energy as though I were in my bedroom with my back holding the door against some robber or worse.

"That's right, Casey. Hold it shut!" Marmor encouraged me.

19

Sweat was pouring out of my body. Holding back empty space turned out to be an exhausting endeavor. I was apparently succeeding, but sometimes it seemed like the 'door' was going to swing open anyway, so I grew increasingly irate. I lashed out, "Why don't the other Wardens come and help?"

"They would help if they could. Don't you know that there are always doors to hold shut and doors to hold open, and they are all and always as urgent as these? These doors are within my domain of responsibility, so it is my appointed duty to hold them shut—or open them, when the time is right!"

I was impressed that he could get all that out while holding shut the gate. I noticed now that he was working hard, but it wasn't nearly as hard for him as it was for me. I realized suddenly that *he* was made for this kind of work. It was all in a day's work for him. What kind of work was I made for?

All the while, my parents continued to work just a few dozen yards away, and the earlier-me continued to wander the yard in abject boredom.

"What is trying to come through?" I gasped as dollops of sweat fell over my eyes.

"They are not what you would call 'the good guys,'" Marmor said, his face taking on a smile for the first time I had known him.

"Why are they here at all?" I pressed.

"Why do they ever come after any human? To bend them to their will. To enslave them. To consume them. No doubt, however, they have learned of your special privilege. A human that can See would be a valuable asset to the Enemy. The Enemy knows that you can See, so they are now here to acquire you."

This made my heart shrink in cold fear, but my mind reeled. Apparently, we humans were targets, and I had risen in importance in their eyes.

"But if they 'acquired' me before I could 'See,' then I wouldn't yet be able to 'See.' Doesn't my presence here right now holding back this gate indicate that they won't get me? Isn't there something here about violating space-time continuums and all that jazz?" I gasped out.

"That's Hollywood nonsense," Marmor retorted. "This is

high theology." Before I could reply, Marmor abruptly stepped away from his gate, and it burst open in flashes of blinding light of all colors. Six golden men, or something like men, stepped into the clearing. They were each at least ten feet tall. They had swords... or their arms *were* swords... I couldn't tell... they were immense, and beautiful, and fearsome, and...

"Step away from the gate!" Marmor ordered.

I did more than step. I collapsed to the ground in sheer exhaustion. The gate swung open, and a mixture of heavenly scent and rotten flesh came pouring out into the clearing. Something stepped over me, then another, and another. I could feel their going—and smell each one. I closed my eyes. I did not want to see them. Finally, curiosity got the best of me. I braved a glimpse and saw thick, dark smudges thrown against the relief of the landscape. They were roughly shaped like bodies, but looked more like large black scabs, oozing puss and blood. They assembled to face the golden men with their swaying swords. I closed my eyes again.

It was over quickly. The golden men spoke a single golden word in unison and the legion of scabs were sent hurtling back over me and tumbling through the gate, howling in pain and anger. I opened my eyes again in time to see the golden men themselves stepping over me on their way through the gate, presumably to chase the scabs back to wherever it was they came from. The last of them put his hand on my shoulder and breathed some comforting word. I immediately took heart. The gate closed. All the smells of before were now replaced by the loveliest smell I think I've ever smelled: freshly baked bread... from heaven? Yes, from heaven. That's my story, and I'm sticking to it. It was a lovely aroma, and like the breathed word, it had the effect of strengthening me.

Marmor was sitting down in the grass at the edge of the wood. A wide smile creased his face.

"Well done, Casey. Well done," he said.

I closed my eyes and fell asleep.

# Chapter 6

I slept a long time. I came awake before I let my eyes open. I was struck at how vivid my dreams had been. Previously, my dreams had always centered on areas within my experience. Wardens! How was any of what I had just gone through related to my life to this point? Bigfoot, as seen in grainy videos on *National Geographic*, yes. Hairy creatures that travel through space and time as gatekeepers—not even on my radar.

I opened my eyes. My brothers were bumbling about the room getting ready for school. Normally, they'd be shoving me around and I'd be resenting it, but right now I would have welcomed even their abrasive treatment. The familiar smells of breakfast cooking floated through the doorway. Vivid or not, one can always tell the difference between dreams and real life. My feet found the floor and I stepped into the hallway to greet my parents. Dream or not, the homesickness I felt was quite real, and I wanted to say good morning to my parents.

"Good morning," I said, stepping past someone in the hallway.

Wait just a minute! I had just said 'good morning' to myself!

I turned on my heels to follow myself back into the bedroom.

"Hey! Can you hear me? Don't you see me?" I called out in a panic.

"Our life is no dream, but it should and will perhaps become one," Marmor said quietly from his spot on one of my brother's bed. I hadn't noticed him.

"It wasn't a dream?" I asked him.

"Wouldn't you mean, 'Isn't *this* a dream?'" he poked.

"Yes, I suppose that is what I mean. I was sleeping, right? I remember sleeping..."

"Yes, you slept. You were exhausted from your effort at the gate. I carried you here thinking a rest in your own bed would be more comfortable than out in the grass."

"This *has* to be a dream," I protested.

"I hate to break it to you," Marmor said, rising, "but even if it *was* a dream, it doesn't follow that it was *necessarily* a *mere* figment of your imagination."

"Some dreams are real, you're saying?"

"*All* dreams are real. If they weren't real, how would you experience them at all? Interaction with the non-existent is not logically possible. Even the innovations of our imagination have, in their elementary parts, some basis in reality. As far as our dreams go, sometimes they are less real than reality in that they are images, or two dimensional representations of reality. But even a picture of a coffee cup is real, even if you wouldn't dare think of putting 'real' coffee in it," Marmor explained, leading me outside.

"Less real?" I scratched my head.

"And sometimes dreams are *just as real* as reality as you experience it, and sometimes even they are *more* real," Marmor continued. "Whether or not that is the case would depend on *who* the dream-giver is."

"Perhaps I am just insane?" I asked him, half jokingly.

"Well, dismissing aspects of your experience as not being real just because they are not as substantive as other aspects of your reality is surely one step down the road to insanity, where insanity is defined as having beliefs that thoroughly do not conform to reality," Marmor instructed, leading me back to the gates we kept the day before.

"Hmmmm," I said, raising my hand. "Hi, my name is Casey. I remind you that I am only twelve."

"I think we can dispense with the notion that the normal limitations of twelve-year-old humans applies to you, but I will yet concede it is still an issue. Even so, your young age is not your only disadvantage. Your race is limited to experiencing only five dimensions. My race lives and breathes in eleven. These concepts are not foreign to us. They are as self-evident to us as what they call 'gravity' is to you," Marmor explained.

"My dad has talked about there being other dimensions. They come up on television sometimes because he watches science fiction shows," I defended myself.

"Yes, well, what is interesting is how easily certain members within your race will tolerate discussions of other dimensions so long as they are seen in wholly naturalistic terms. But what is the spiritual except another dimension? Ah, but that would be to admit something that is unacceptable. Typical humans: accepting reality, but only on their own terms. In short, not accepting reality at all."

"I hope you will be explaining more," I told him, not really grasping what he was saying.

"I will, as I am able. These are not yet the 'deep things.' You are twelve years old, which is young in human terms. I am some two hundred years old, which is young for Wardens. I have only spoken of that which I have directly experienced, just as you might speak about your daily interactions with light and motion. The elders can explain more to you when you are able to receive it," Marmor said.

I was silent.

"Take my hand," Marmor ordered. I obeyed. "Hold on."

Instantly, the world around me was obscured. I was enveloped in bright white light and heat and the pleasant smell of freshly baked bread. A fair moment later, I found myself standing with Marmor in an open expanse of glistening white light in all directions. Think of a room painted white on all sides, including the floor—now take out the walls and ceilings, and imagine that the white plane went on infinitely.

"Where are we?" I asked him.

"Shhhhhh."

Marmor was waiting for something. I waited with him.

After a few moments, the space began pulsating. The ground vibrated. There was a shaking. From above, a blinding object like the sun began to descend. The smell of bread cooking intensified; it was as if my nostrils were ovens, and the bread was baking from within them. It was heavenly and terrible all at the same time. I closed my eyes and shielded them with my hands. Despite this, I could see flashes of light streaking across my eyelids. Hold a flashlight to your finger—it glows red. Light can get through anything if it is bright enough. You can even see through your own eyelid and even, I discovered, your hand. I heard thunder, and felt its violence in my heart.

Then it all came to a stop. While it was still painful, I opened my eyes. Before me was a mighty host of the beings that had come through the gate in defense of my house and home, and

24

apparently, me.

"This is real," Marmor informed me.

"What is it?" I trembled.

"It was from this place that the Dragon was cast out."

"Why am I here?" I moaned. The glory of the place was unbearable. I ached in all places.

"So you can understand, or at least have a glimpse of understanding. The Prowling Lion desires to have you and make you his slave. You, and the rest of your race. Here before you is the army that serves endlessly to resist them in that effort. They go to and fro, exerting themselves always on your behalf. The Wardens do the same, only they are bound to your five dimensions more intricately. These messengers are not bound to five or eleven dimensions. They are bound to many more that I do not comprehend. The higher the dimension the being, the lower they can descend. The cup of coffee can be rendered as an image and the coffee with it. But the image can never hold the 'real coffee.' New wineskins for new wine: 'in a flash, in the twinkling of an eye,' that is what you and your race waits for, and what the hosts of heaven and the Lord's Army, which I belong to, prepares you for every moment of every day—a fact your race is blissfully and constantly unaware of."

"It is too much!" I cried out. "Take me from here!"

Instantly I was standing in another grassy clearing, Marmor near at hand. I exhaled deeply in relief.

"For a little while, my friend Casey," Marmor said solemnly. "You are in the Lord's service in a manner that you were not created for. In the natural order, the angels serve you, and the Wardens serve you by serving the angels. For the moment, your task is to enter into my work, the duty of the Wardens, and serve the angels. Never before has such a thing happened. You are a marked man, but His seal over you is sure."

"It is too much!" I declared.

"It *is*; that is all there is to it," Marmor rejoined.

I sobbed, "I just want to go home! I want to eat eggs and drink milk and play in my yard and hug my mother!" I was crying like a child, but I didn't care.

Marmor's eyes softened, "You are already on your way home.

You just don't know it. If you were flying in from Paris, you would appreciate the fact that it takes a certain amount of time that cannot be avoided, and you simply must take a form of transport, what with all its strengths and limitations. You can't just skip it, close your eyes in Paris and open them a second later and find yourself safe in bed. You must make the journey. It is like that, now. On account of what has happened, you must follow this path, for as long as it must go on, in the way that it must take."

"It is too much," I said again, regaining my composure.

"Even so, we must do our duty," he said, taking my arm.

"Where are we going?" I asked wearily.

"Three days from now and a hundred miles away, the Enemy will be descending in force on a little girl's room in a brutal attempt to enslave her. If we don't go now, we won't make it in time!" he said, stepping up to a gate that I hadn't noticed before.

My weariness disappeared and my resolve stiffened. I should like to have gone home to my comfortable bed, but even I could see that service in the Lord's Army would mean, ultimately, intense gratification. How often do twelve-year-olds get to offer their bodies as shields for others?

"How often, indeed," Marmor said, pulling me through the gate.

Then, light. And the scent of baked bread.

# Chapter 7

Through the white tunnels again. Marmor walked briskly and I struggled to keep up. The elegant etchings bore witness to exploits and achievements I couldn't comprehend. The glassy walls with their chiseled stories spoke to the great deeds of the Wardens, and I felt a little sad that I could not perceive the victories described on them. Marmor continued on, swiftly.

"Marmor! You said we had three days!" I protested, hoping he would slow down.

"Weren't you listening to me? Time happens differently for us. I said we had to go now, or else we wouldn't make it!" Marmor argued over his shoulder.

I mumbled something I hoped he didn't hear and trudged on in a steady jog.

Marmor stopped in front of a place in the wall that I was beginning to recognize bore peculiar markings that meant, 'Here is a gate!'

"Here is a gate!" Marmor confirmed.

"I thought you said we had to travel hundreds of miles! We've only been walking... well, you've been walking, I've been running... for an hour!" I objected breathlessly.

"I was sure that you were listening to me before. Next time I will look to make sure," Marmor sighed. "Now, about this girl..."

But Marmor had to wait because I was bent over, wheezing.

"Are you composed?" he asked after a moment, inclining his head in concern.

"Tell me about the girl," I said.

"This is no ordinary girl," Marmor began, his voice taking a solemn tone.

"In what way?" I prodded, after he hadn't continued his account for a moment.

"Ok," Marmor said, apparently having collected his thoughts better. "Truth be told, there are no ordinary people. Every one of you is remarkable. Every last one of you is royalty. That said, your import on the affairs of your world varies. Usually, no human is aware of their impact, whether it is great or small, and many a human has thought they were of great importance when in fact they were of very little, and many who were deemed of little import are profoundly influential, for better or for worse. Who can measure this but God? Yet sometimes we Wardens can wager a guess."

"How?"

"Over whom the angels contend greatly, we surmise they are of import. Over whom they tend to lightly, we surmise that perhaps they are not so much; at least, not yet."

"That makes sense," I said, reasoning it out.

"You will remember how we rushed to your residence to hold back the angels of darkness until the angels of light had arrived. You remember the number of those involved. You, Casey, are truly of import. You are the apple of His eye, as your entire race is, but you are of import in a way that many of them are not... yet."

I felt a blush creeping into my cheeks as I pondered my alleged importance. Just then, Marmor threw open the gate and pulled me through.

A large white farmhouse, appearing like a manor, was the first thing to catch my attention. It was only for a moment, though, as there was a flurry of activity all around it. Everywhere I looked there were Wardens with their backs against pulsating gates. There must have been a hundred Wardens striving mightily to hold back the Enemy hordes. They were on the ground, in the trees, on the roof... some even seemed to be suspended in midair, pushing against nothing to hold back the invading danger. More disconcerting than that—which was already pretty disconcerting!—was the fact that there were strewn about the limp bodies of fallen Wardens; the gates they had been holding were flung open, some seeming almost to be hanging from threads. In the margins between the gates and the house, dozens, if not hundreds, if not *thousands* of angels and fallen angels fought against each other in a display simultaneously hideous and awesome.

"We are late! They are through!" I cried out.

"Do you think this battle began moments ago? No. It is always engaged. The angels are always contending for this young girl. The contest began long before I was born and will continue until He Rides the Clouds," Marmor explained calmly.

I was confused and surprised. "What are we to do, then?"

"The gate that is ours to hold is inside the house. Come. We have made it just in time."

Marmor strode briskly to the house. A quick walk for him required a sprint from me. Once at the house, Marmor disappeared inside of it, passing through the closed door. When I arrived, I put my hand on the door to feel if it was really there. It really was. "Marmor?" I called out hesitatingly.

A hairy arm reached through the hardness of the door and yanked me through it.

"Sorry about that," Marmor said.

"Uh, we'll have to talk about what just happened there some time," I muttered. Passing through something I had just established as a real, tangible object didn't hurt or feel unpleasant, but it was still unnerving.

"Come," Marmor instructed.

Marmor didn't wait to see if I was following. He turned away from me and ascended a lovely spiral staircase that was in the foyer. I, however, fell backwards against the hard door in startled amazement: the spiral stair case wrapped around the trunk of a massive tree that shot up through and into the house. The thick limbs went off in all directions and were enmeshed and intertwined with the walls and ceiling of the house. Occasionally, branches hung down into the rooms that I could see around me. Regaining my composure, I rushed up the stairs.

As I mounted the second floor, I could see that the tree and the house were a single, living organism. The limbs were not just supporting the structure, but were part of the structure. From the second floor I could see more of the hanging branches out towards the edge of the house. The leaves were bright and green and seemed to be speckled with snow. The apparent snowflakes made the leaves appear to glisten when a wind rose to blow them gently. I felt no wind, personally, but the tree nonetheless seemed to sway slightly. At times I could even feel the floor beneath me move, ever so slightly.

Marmor stuck his head out of a door down one of the long

halls. "Come!" he ordered.

I hastened down the hallway and into the room Marmor had beckoned me into.

To this point I had been so overwhelmed from the total experience—being yanked through a closed door into a house that was a tree and a tree that was a house—that I hadn't yet taken note of the décor. One could not escape noticing it inside the room, however. Here I could see that branches protruded briefly up out of the floor to transform itself into the shape of furniture. Really old furniture. Really old furniture that was grand, spanking new. Wrap your head around that! The whole room looked like something out of colonial times, except that every item looked like it had been made just yesterday. It wasn't a room one would find on the frontier, either. It was an upper class, Georgian-era style room. On reflection, the whole house bore resemblance to the colonial mansions I had seen in my brief lifetime.

Marmor was kneeling next to a bed. On that bed was the oldest woman I had ever seen. She was hopelessly frail. Her skin hung like thin paper on her bones. Her head had spatterings of gray hair here and there, but in the main, she was bald. I saw now that Marmor was holding her hand. I drew close to the foot of the bed and leaned against an ornate dresser. I perceived that Marmor had brought me to this woman's death bed, and to say I was uncomfortable would be an understatement.

"Come, Myrtle," Marmor said, "take and eat."

But Myrtle merely turned her head away from Marmor. Whether it was in stubbornness, or in death, I did not know.

"Myrtle, take and eat," Marmor said again.

"Marmor," I said in a hushed tone, "where is the little girl we are to help?"

"She is the one you see lying before us," Marmor stated.

Silence. I could feel the house creaking beneath me and sensed it swaying in the wind, its many leaves serving as a sail. After a few moments I felt a shudder go through the house. This felt different than the previous movements—more like an earthquake—and I looked around nervously.

The shriveled old lady turned in her bed so as to now face Marmor and myself.

30

"Let me go. Let me die. Let them come," the bony woman pleaded.

"You know that you won't die, Myrtle. *You know it*," Marmor pleaded.

"Let them come," the woman said again.

"That they have already been here is clear enough," Marmor sighed.

We sat there for a moment or so in the quiet. The woman had pulled her hand away from Marmor's as she made her last remark. It now seemed as though she was clutching her heart with it. Her ancient face was drawn up in creaking pain. Her eyes roamed the room, aimlessly. When they were turned once towards me, I saw that they were dark, bottomless pits. I had not previously known that despair could take on a flesh. Myrtle showed that it could, and did.

"It is time," Marmor said quietly, standing. "Casey, you will help."

"Yes, anything, Marmor."

"Here is the gate. Do you see it?"

I looked in the direction he was pointing at. It was near the foot of the bed, about three feet off the ground. It was hard to spot a gate, even if one had eyes to see it. The border of the gate was like a single strand of a spider's web. It caught the light, however, even when there was no light, so if you knew what to look for, you could often spot the edges of a gate.

"They are coming. Put your back up against it. There is room for me to do the same," Marmor instructed.

With that, we both put our backs against the invisible door. I could feel it trembling as the Enemy drew closer. I knew the Enemy had arrived, however, when the gate bulged against my back. My feet looked for traction as I sought to push back against the interlopers. One foot found one of the legs of the bed, and I fought back earnestly. Marmor was exerting himself heavily, too. On occasion, the gate would open a crack, and I would smell rotten flesh. The attack persisted longer than previous times, and I began to worry that the Lord's Army would not come, or would come too late.

After a time, Marmor's eyes lit up. "The battle is engaged!" he

31

shouted.

"I don't understand. They are still on the other side of the gate," I expressed my confusion.

"Yes, that's right. The Lord's Army contends with the Enemy on the other side of the gate. When the Lord's Army gains the upper hand, we will open the gate so that they can perform their vital ministry," he explained.

The battle went on for a long time. On occasion, the gate would shiver behind me, and I could feel it try to swing out. I would push back all the more. I became acutely aware of the sounds of the contest. There had always been what seemed like the sounds of thunder and crashing, but in the scheme of things the events had been too short-lived for them to register. Now I felt that I was at the heart of a tempest. The whole room vibrated with the sounds and force of the storm that was just a slender sliver of time and space away. Myrtle rested in clear discomfort but didn't seem to be aware of what was going on just a few feet away.

"The tide has turned," Marmor declared. He hesitated another moment and then issued the order, "Step aside!"

I was a sweaty mess and truly exhausted. I obeyed the command with relief. I shakily found a chair nearby. I noticed that, like every other object in the room, despite its old style it bore all the signs of being brand new. It held my weight easily as I panted heavily.

The gate flung open and out tumbled three or four angels of God still grappling with one of the Enemy. They rolled about on the floor some as a few more angels stepped through the gate, guarding it diligently and carefully monitoring the situation before them. At last, the Enemy angel was subdued. Each of the Lord's Soldiers took hold of a corner of him and threw him with blinding force back through the gate... which Marmor then slammed shut.

Now I beheld the angels, seven in number, come around the bedside of decrepit Myrtle. Before their presence clouded my view of her, I saw her turn from them in resolute stubbornness, but as she was now surrounded on all sides, there was no escape for her roving eyes. In every direction they turned, I knew, she would see them. Even if she closed her eyes, the paper-thin skin would not be able to block out their glory.

"The real battle now begins," Marmor said between gasping breaths. He too was exhausted. He sunk down on the floor beside me and sat cross-legged with his back against the room's wall.

"Now what?" I asked.

"We pray," he replied.

"For what? The angels have already been sent and have already arrived," I said.

"Yes, but the task is this: He must melt her heart without breaking it. He could Conquer and take what He wants by Conquest, but it is His choice to win her back by wooing. So you see, just as He has decided to honor and respect the boundaries of human will, which He Himself has set, so too has He decided to take power and permission from the pleas, in prayer, of we His creation. I do not understand it, but the command is clear... 'Pray continually.' So let us pray."

Marmor closed his eyes then and prayed.

Not sure what exactly I was praying for, I closed my eyes as well, and in my heart I said, "Dear God, help Myrtle with whatever she is supposed to do, and help those who have been sent to her side do what is necessary to help her."

After the first few minutes of offered prayer, I dozed off. An hour went by. Then two. Ok, I really don't know how much time passed. When my eyes finally opened and stayed open, the great canopy of angelic arms still concealed Myrtle from my sight. Marmor was standing where he had previously been sitting, with his back still against the wall. His eyes glinted with expectation, and the room seemed to be charged with a new atmosphere. It had felt before as though Death itself had its heavy hand on the room. I wouldn't say that Life now bore the room up, but Death at least had apparently departed.

Finally, I sensed some real activity. One of the angels near the center of the bed stepped back and gestured in my direction. Myrtle's old eyes settled on me. I felt their weight on me. They had softened a great deal and there was now definite intelligence in them, but it was unnerving, nonetheless. I squirmed. I knew it was rude, but I squirmed.

A moment later, another of the angels moved from his place. He strode across the room to a vanity where he picked up what seemed to be a serving plate with a clear, glass cover. I could see that there was only one item on the plate. It was about the size and shape of a strawberry, but it was white and sparkled like a diamond. It was so remarkable that I couldn't believe I hadn't noticed it before.

The plate was brought to Myrtle's bedside.

"Take and eat," the angel said.

"What is that?" I whispered to Marmor.

Marmor, who was smiling, said, "It is the last fruit of this Season. It is now nearly spoiled. If she doesn't eat of it now, there won't be another harvest for a time, time and a half, and half a time."

"But, what is it?"

Marmor only smiled.

# Chapter 8

Myrtle reached out her hand and took the pure white 'strawberry' in her weak grasp. Beneath her gown I could see faintly the spindly arms and the bony elbow bend as she put the fruit near her mouth. She hesitated; the faces of the angelic beings were taut with expectation, and I could literally feel their heightened concern. Marmor was smiling, the only one in the room who was. It was as if he knew something that no one else, not even the Lord's Army, knew. Myrtle bit into the fruit once, then twice, and with the third bite it disappeared entirely.

She laid back against the pillow, and a look of mirth stole across the face of the angels. They began singing, though softly, a hymn. Myrtle recognized it and smiled, looking from one brilliant face to the other.

"Watch," Marmor said.

Myrtle's body began to shimmer, reflecting a light from an unknown source. It was not a blinding light akin to the light that the angels emitted, but it wouldn't be right to characterize it as 'glowing.' The light seemed alive. It slowly consumed her as she had consumed the fruit until I couldn't see her at all. Then, pushing out of the contours of the light, were Myrtle's arms and legs. Her body was growing so that it overtook the light; her body passed it by as it were, and it was soon behind her—behind her skin and behind her flesh. Where there had been just skin pulled tightly over skinny bones with no rise and fall at the joints there was now flesh and form. Her head, which had previously shown only occasional patches of wiry gray hair now grew out long black strands of shiny new hair. It didn't take long before her hair resembled that of a young woman, falling perfectly down around her shoulders.

And Myrtle was becoming a young woman to match that hair, right before my eyes.

Where previously her eyes had peered out of bony sockets, there was now flesh and eyebrows. Her lips no longer looked parched and her cheeks became rosy. There was a sparkle in her eyes. No doubt, it was the light that her body had consumed escaping from its lamp-holes. She was smiling with joy uncon-

35

strained.

While her face was filling out, I noticed that the rest of her body was, too. I blushed as I realized that while previously the person on the bed resembled a perfectly straight, dried stick with a robe thrown over it, there were now curves. There were shapes. I covered my eyes.

When I opened them a moment later at Marmor's nudging, I saw that Myrtle had thrown another garment over her robe. Nonetheless, where there had just a moment ago been the oldest woman I had ever seen—that *anyone* had ever seen—there was now the most beautiful young woman that I had ever seen… that *anyone* had ever seen. I was not good at guessing ages even in normal circumstances, but I would wager that she appeared to be not more than eighteen or nineteen years old.

She stood and approached me and I did what seemed right: I fell to my knees and reached out to take her hand to kiss it, as this seemed the proper thing to do when meeting a queen. Myrtle apparently agreed, for her hand was there for me to take and kiss. Out of the corner of my eye, I saw that Marmor was kneeling as well.

"Now you begin to understand why we kneel," Marmor murmured enigmatically.

"Stand up, son, stand up," Myrtle ordered me, taking my hand in hers and pulling me to my feet. I tried to lift my face to see her eye to eye, but I couldn't. I knew I was blushing again because my cheeks felt hot. I looked down at my feet. My knees shook as if they knew on their own that the right place for me to be was on them, honoring and worshiping…

Well, the word that comes to mind is 'goddess.' I suppose everyone has seen beautiful women before, but you cannot imagine just how glorious Myrtle had become in this moment. From this moment on, all claims to wonder and beauty would be compared against the person of Myrtle, and would pale in comparison. I can't explain it except to say that my heart burned inside of me, and my blood sped throughout my body, like water coursing through a canyon, my soul borne up by the rapids beneath me. And this is not a sufficient explanation at all.

"Son," she said. "Stand up. Look at me."

I tried to find words, "It hurts…"

"It'll get easier. Look at me, son."

If Myrtle, the ancient-heap-of-bones, had called me son I could have understood the gesture and the endearment it contained, but Myrtle the eighteen-year-old saying it simply unnerved me. In what respect could I possibly be her son? If she had said to me, "Stand, child," I might have been a little indignant, but I could have understood the logic.

"My son," she said, running her hand through my hair, lifting my head. Her eyes, I saw, brimmed with an affection for me that I just couldn't fathom. "Pull those chairs over," she ordered Marmor.

Marmor grabbed the chair I had been sitting on and another nearby and lifted them into the air. To my surprise, the legs of the chairs, though clearly resembling an old colonial style, had in fact been alive! When the chair left the ground, the branches of the tree that had been the legs fell back into the floor like a fish falling back into a lake. When Marmor set it back down near the bed, branches reached up out of the floor to take hold and graft themselves back into it. I saw now that all of the items in the room were alive in this way. I confess that I was now actually becoming afraid. What had I gotten myself into? Why did I foolishly try to win a piece of hair from Big Foot? Clearly I had ventured where even the angels are afraid to tread!

We were now all three sitting facing each other. Myrtle was on the bed, and Marmor and I were each poised in our own chairs. The angels had disappeared, their going evidenced only by the distant scent of a bakery. Myrtle reached her hand out and took mine and held it throughout the conversation that followed.

"So, Marmor. You are more clever than I guessed," she said to him.

"I assure you, my dearest queen, that I did not arrange this," he commented.

"Oh? I should like to hear some time how another mere mortal has come to See… I presume that he has not eaten of the Tree?" she asked, cocking her head quizzically.

"No, my Lady. His sight came as a special dispensation

granted by Mammal," Marmor explained.

"Very interesting. Very interesting, indeed. I will hear that story on another day, though," she replied, her velvety voice evoking the splendor of her station.

"You are a very special young man at any rate," she continued, addressing me. "You are my own flesh and blood, though it may seem to you distantly."

"You... you... are my mother?" I wondered.

"Distantly, as I said. Your mother is a beautiful woman, no?" she asked.

As a matter of fact, only the week before I had been reflecting on this very fact. The evening's ruminations then had begun by contemplating my realization that many of my classmates were, well, quite pretty. It wasn't the fact that they were pretty that drove me to thinking, but the fact that this was something that I had now noticed. In the course of considering that issue, I thought about the mothers of my classmates and couldn't bring myself to think that they were pretty, too. But that evening when I saw my mother in the kitchen, wearing her rather plain clothes and not even a swipe of makeup, I realized with a start—you cannot imagine my astonishment— that she was rather pretty, even beautiful, as Myrtle had indicated. When my father came home from work, I regarded them both in light of this new discovery. I had stumbled upon something mysterious, but couldn't put my finger on whether this mystery resided within me, or without.

"Yes, ma'am, she is," I agreed.

"As only to be expected, as she can rightly be called my daughter," Myrtle said.

"Pardon me, ma'am," I stammered, "but I am very confused. Just how old are you?"

Myrtle threw her head back and laughed and laughed. If bells were made of gold, that's what they would sound like when they rang. That was what her laugh sounded like. Even now she did not let go of my hand.

"Old! I'm very old. And now thanks to Marmor and the angels... and to you... I'm very young. Young and old: in the beginning it was not meant that they would be opposites!" Myrtle laughed.

"Please, ma'am…"

"Call me Myrtle, lad. Call me Myrtle."

This was hard to do.

"Please, Myrtle," I forced myself to say, "what did I just witness?"

"That is a very good question and cannot be fully answered. Perhaps this will suffice: I had fallen into complete and utter despair and wished only for the end to come. Unfortunately, it is probably the case for me, as with everyone else, that the end will not come until the great Day of the Lord," Myrtle said.

"You mean, you can't die? You looked awfully close to it," I said, and then catching myself. "Not meaning to be disrespectful…"

Myrtle didn't seem to mind the question. She explained, "Oh, we are all dying. Even me. Minute you're conceived, you're dying. What is 'death' but one particular point on the spectrum of dying? We all carry around our bodies of death, lad. In my case, though, I will never reach that particular point that we customarily call 'death.'"

"That seems like a very good thing," I observed. "Why would you ever fall into despair?"

"When you live and live and live, and the people you love meet Death all the time, and you see the great stain of Death on humanity for generation after generation, you begin to see that while Death and dying are a murderous evil, and an enemy to be defeated. Still, it is a blessing that our race does not have to go on and on, dying a little bit more every day, until, finally, facing the first death. In a single generation I think we all see that miserable stain reach in and out of the lives of those we love and those we don't, but I have seen many generations. I guess I had hoped… or been convinced… or… well, at any rate, I had hoped that maybe, just maybe I could fade away…"

"But you couldn't, and can't," Marmor chided.

"You're right, of course," Myrtle agreed.

"You should have eaten of the fruit again and sustained your strength so that you may have been of good and noble use these last few centuries," Marmor chastened her. "We were down to the last one! Imagine if you had laid there for centuries more until the next harvest. You would not have passed on, and you would have only have become all the more decrepit!"

"Relent and forgive, my friend!" Myrtle cried out. "I cannot contest your words. Yet you Wardens do not understand my curse. You live on and on but you are strong enough to bear it. I have been rejuvenated for a time, but I am still dying. *I am still dying.*" For the first time, something like sadness came across her visage, and I began to cry, for such a look on such a face was a heart-rending thing. It brought me real pain to see anything less than joyous mirth on that lovely face.

Myrtle laughed, unleashing golden peels of ringing bells, and I involuntarily stopped crying and felt again the joy of life. "All is well, my son. It is well," she said.

Having regained my composure, I asked the question that kept pressing in on all sides of my mind, "So just how old *are* you?"

Myrtle merely laughed.

"Alright, then, so you aren't going to answer that one. Tell me, then. What is this fruit that you have eaten?" I asked. This question too had been competing for attention in my mind.

Myrtle laughed all the more, "Dear child! Have you not guessed? It is a fruit of the tree you have been ensconced beneath this entire time. Don't you see? It is the Tree of Life!"

It all became very clear. And I became very afraid.

# Chapter 9

It had only been a few months ago that my father had greeted me when I came home from school and told me that my *real* education was about to begin. On the kitchen table waiting for me were our holy books and many others that I did not expect. There were books on geology and biology and physics and mathematics and literature and lexicons and commentaries. "To understand *that*," my father had said, "you have to read *these*." Seeing the amount of work he had in store for me, I protested, "But dad, shouldn't reading the Bible be enough? Why bother reading other books?" It was a theological objection of sorts that really only masked my laziness, and my father saw right through it: "These books are written using language in specific times and places by real people who lived in their own culture. You cannot hope to read the Bible if you cannot read at all." I argued back, "But, Dad! Why does it even matter? At school they said that all the religions have their own stories. What do *our* stories have to do with today?" After this, my father became silent in apparent shock, and only sporadically did he get me to sit at the table to study.

But Myrtle had eaten of the Tree of Life. It was real. It was all real. *Real.*

I was terrified. I mean, beyond words, terrified.

You might think this a foolish thing to have only realized this now. There were, of course, the Wardens. I had encountered angels, and evidently demons, too, though I hadn't yet laid eyes on one. This should all have served notice to the fact that there was much more to reality than I knew. *Some of the old stories were true.* What if they *all* were? What was I into?

Myrtle seemed to know my thoughts.

"Do not fear, little one," she said.

"Easy for you to say," I murmured.

"You will return to me in time, and you will come to understand more. For now, know that seeing my own precious kin—that's you, Casey—reminded me of the hope that I have. You helped me see that life is worth living, despite its many calamities. Thank you."

Then she took my hand and kissed it, and I trembled as a slave might tremble if his master had knelt before him or if the king kissed the hand of the peasant.

"It is time to go," Marmor said, putting his big hairy hand on my shoulder.

Myrtle waved goodbye to me as I followed Marmor out of the room, and I made a faint attempt to reciprocate. I followed Marmor down the hall and down the spiral stairs. My hand went out on its own accord to touch the bark of the thick tree trunk as I winded my way down. It seemed softer than a tree ought, and a growing sense that a heart beat within it compelled me to pull my probing fingers back, abruptly.

Outside, the battle between angels and demons and Wardens was still going, but it was clear that the enemy agents were enraged at their most recent defeat. They fell further and further away from the house, and this enraged them further. Marmor guided me easily through the lot of them to the place where we had first come upon the scene. I followed him into the white cavernous tunnel, mute. We walked at a pace that could be deemed 'leisurely.' It was the slowest Marmor had ever walked in my presence. Nonetheless, neither of us spoke.

Finally, we emerged in what I instantly knew to be the great hall where I had originally been put on 'trial' by the Warden council. It was easy to surmise since the council was present and in session. The main difference was that rather than being cloaked in a great darkness, the place was brimming with light. Curiosity elbowed its way into my mind, and I was about to ask Marmor whether or not it had always been so bright, but he quickly led me to the center of the hall. At this point, the council stood and faced me and knelt down before me again as though I were a king—an absurd thing to do.

After an interminable amount of time, they returned to their places.

"It has been a pleasure and an experience having one of the Sons of Adam among us in this special way. We would remind him that our existence must be kept a secret. It must be told to no one but those who already know. Our existence is endangered enough," King Mammal said.

"Am I.... Am I going home?" I stuttered.

"Indeed you are," King Mammal smiled.

"I thought I was going to have to be with you a lot longer. Not that I am complaining," I quickly added.

"You do not quite realize how long you have been here," he returned.

Before I could respond to that, several Wardens entered the hall with a cart full of tools.

"Our artisans," Marmor informed me.

No one spoke as the artisans set upon one of the columns near where the king's throne was. They worked so quickly and efficiently that I couldn't imagine that they were doing a very good job, but in short order they had their cart loaded up and they departed. King Mammal gestured to me to come and see.

On the column was etched in exquisite detail a room that I knew instantly was Myrtle's. A series of panels showed a young boy sitting across from an old woman lying in a bed. As the panels progressed, the woman gained her strength, reached out and took the fruit and ate, and gained her victory. The young boy was depicted as holding up her faltering hand as she stretched out her arm to take the fruit. Nowhere in any of the panels was there a hint of any angelic warriors or Marmor, who had been there the entire time.

"It is not accurate!" I declared.

"It *is* accurate," King Mammal replied, nonplussed.

"But I just sat there. Everyone else did all the work! I should not get any of the credit!" I protested.

"Now you know the way of the Wardens. To God be the Glory, and to Him whom He has glorified, and to those through Him He has glorified; the Wardens are content with this," King Mammal explained patiently. I suddenly remembered that the first time I was in this hall there were some Wardens that did not seem to quite accept this view of things. But the King was continuing.

"It is time for you to return to your family, Casey," the King said. "Go in peace."

With that, Marmor led me away. We wound our way through the crystal spaces for a time until we had at last apparently reached our destination.

"We will meet again, my friend," Marmor said, touching both my shoulders with his hands. He towered over me, of course. I hugged him. This seemed to make him uncomfortable, and I thought I could understand the sentiment after meeting Myrtle. The plain light of the sun suddenly appeared, and a doorway opened up before me. I felt Marmor's hand at my back as I stepped through the fissure. I stepped out onto the green grass near my shed. I turned to wave to Marmor, but he was gone. There was no sign of a doorway cut out of the sky, either.

Not knowing what else to do, I stood there for a time.

Then I spotted the jar.

"Aha!" I shouted, pouncing on it. I picked it up and examined the ground for pebbles. There turned out to be a great many of them and I quickly gave up any hope of finding the place where everything had first begun.

"Casey!" a man's voice distracted me from my quest.

"Hi, Dad!" I said in excitement. I really had begun to miss my family.

"Come on in. We're about to have dinner!" my dad replied.

"Did you miss me?" I asked him.

He looked at me, confused, "Miss you?"

"I've been gone a week at least. Probably more!" I said, hurt a little that my absence hadn't been noticed.

He laughed, "What are you playing at, son? You only just walked out the door a minute ago, and I saw you meander over to the shed! You dawdle like the best of them, but that was no week!"

It was then I realized that I had returned to the very moment that I had first left. The Warden-king had been correct: I didn't realize how long I had been gone. Not long at all! I followed my dad into the house. My brothers and sisters were all about the place, setting the table, squabbling, and otherwise making progress towards supper.

Sydney came barreling down the hall in her customary way. She elbowed past me. I felt my blood temperature rise... and told myself that she was only seven. "She's only seven," I repeated to myself. "Only seven." Sydney, of course, hadn't even noticed me as she pushed by me. I found myself actually smiling about it.

The table was set. The eight place settings were all there, even if they were in disarray. Somehow half of the glasses hadn't made it to the table, so I retrieved some more and put them down. Five-year-old Jessica was saying, "I put the cups on, Mom. I did it all by myself." I thought to myself that I ought to correct her and alert Mother to the fact that I had pitched in, but another thought came quickly on the heels of that one urging me to let it go, which I did.

We sat down to eat. It was noisy as always but not nearly as annoying. I spied the pile of books that Dad had set out for me several months ago. We had only gone through them five or six times since, as I had resisted the whole business. I regarded them with new interest, but that old laziness returned as I saw again how thick each of them were. Still, they seemed to call to me in a fresh way.

"Dad?" I queried.

"Yes?" he replied from the other side of the table.

I nodded to the books nearby, "It's real, you know. It's all *real*."

He smiled.

Between bites of my salad, the smells of dinner filled up my nostrils. I realized that I hadn't eaten the entire time that I was away. I had never felt hungry, but I had taken the simple pleasure of eating for granted. Never again!

"Mom, that bread smells great!" I said, looking around eagerly for the fresh baked loaf.

"But, son," she said, with eyes twinkling merrily, "I didn't make any bread tonight."

# Chapter 10

What has life been like since my time with Marmor and meeting Myrtle? You cannot imagine how I watch the shadows. Every sudden flash of light, say, in a reflection, rouses my attention and calls forth from within me the deep pangs of homesickness I had previously experienced in longing to be back with my family. Wherever I stepped, I expected mystery to leap out. All of my daily trials remained, but my attitude was such that I never grew impatient. Except, I was disappointed that nothing marvelous ever unfolded before my eyes. A lurking sense that the marvelous was occurring outside my detection tormented me. Only by holding in my head the proposition that the marvelous was all around me whether I see it or not was I able to keep back despair, for my ordinary life seemed dull in comparison to the extraordinary life I knew others were living. Day by day, my remembrances of that extraordinary life, which I had briefly enjoyed, faded. There was a growing temptation to dismiss it all as a dream, but I fought it, knowing it was just that, a temptation. In the meantime, I no longer regarded myself, or the people around me, in a worldly way.

My family noticed the change immediately. I bent over backwards to express respect and gratitude for my parents. I was more patient with my siblings. Initially, at least, I showed some willingness to read some of the books my father had laid out for me. A theory had developed in my mind that ours was a royal line.

How else to explain Myrtle's comments about my mother and me being her children? This, I suppose, made me a prince. What kingdom were we to rule? I hoped my studies would point me in the right direction. At any rate, I found myself in awe of my parents, and even a little of my siblings. We all were such that Wardens bowed low before us. Angelic hosts contended over us. There wasn't just more to reality than I had previously understood. There was more to being human.

As time went on, though, my enthusiasm waned. Reading dense books was hard work, and who wanted to do hard work when the rest of my friends were playing video games or out riding bikes? As my experiences receded further into the past, so too did my interest in thinking about them.

About three months after my return home, my parents woke us up early in the morning and instructed us to get dressed in our Sunday best. We were going to a funeral.

"Who died, Mama?" little Sydney asked.

"You don't know her," Father said.

"But she was a very special woman," Mother inserted.

Soon we were packed into the van for the two hour trip. To my surprise, the funeral was not being held at a funeral home. Instead, we headed out into the country. Deep woods with emerald leaves engulfed us. On occasion, the forest would give way, and we'd see fields and farms. Then the trees would again overtake us. They stretched up high above us on both sides, and their limbs reached across the road to shake hands with their neighbors. The effect for us was a dark green tunnel.

Evidently, it had been a long time since my parents had been wherever it was we were going, because my mother was constantly consulting a map and providing 'suggestions' to my father on where to go. His lips were drawn tight across his face, and he answered her only in mumblings and grunts. It was clear that we had arrived, however, when we were forced to slow down on account of the traffic jam—in the middle of the wilderness.

Cars were parked in both directions on either side of the country road for as long as I could see.

"Hmmm. We'd better just park here," said Father.

Throwing the van in reverse, he maneuvered his way onto the apron of the road and parked. We had the door open before the van had stopped. The first thing I noticed was a war between scents. On the one hand, I smelled earth, trees, and flowers. On the other hand, I smelled lunch. Something delightful was being cooked not too far away. Roasted meats, to be sure, but also cookies or cake!

"This will be the best funeral ever, I think," young Jessica remarked.

"Hush, Jessica," Mother said, aghast. "We've got to be respectful. Someone dear has died."

When our mother was out of sight, Tom, my oldest brother,

said, "I think Jess has it right."

We all thought Jess had it right. The pleasant smells drew us on, and we walked hastily to find their source. This required making a pretty long walk along the side of the road, with cars moving slowly beside us. We moved slowly with the crowd, bunching up periodically like an accordion, folding and unfolding, as movement started and stopped. It took thirty minutes just to get to the driveway, where things sped up a great deal. The driveway bent in a gentle semi-circle, concealing our destination.

At last, the tunnel of trees disintegrated and we were standing in a large clearing. A field with tall grasses rose up to my left, and to the right was a large well-manicured lawn that was occupied by several thousand people and white folding chairs. Near the house, row after row of tables stood decked out with the food to feed us all. But my attention was riveted on the house.

It was a tall, stately manor-like farmhouse that I knew in my gut had to be Myrtle's. When Marmor and I had first seen the house, it had been from a different perspective. It didn't exactly match my recollection, but I *knew* it had to be Myrtle's house. My heart fell within me as I remembered that we were here for a funeral. Young, pristine Myrtle had died after all! Against my will, I began to cry.

"But, Casey, I don't think you knew Myrtle?" Father asked me, gazing at me curiously.

I stifled a sob and emitted an incoherent answer that neither of us understood.

Mother came and put her arm around me as my siblings cast perplexed and even humored glances at me. "Death is a terrible thing. It's OK to cry about it, Casey, so long as we remember that it's a *defeated* thing," she said.

Maxwell, my older brother of fifteen and the twin of Samuel, elbowed me as he strode past me, "Still, maybe you'd want to at least see the dead body first?"

I didn't even have the energy to glower at him. Mother escorted me down the lane to the front of the house. Father corralled my siblings, "We must go and introduce ourselves and give our condolences and then find a seat for all of us, and then we can split up and explore."

We climbed the steps and stood in a line that stretched around the side of the house on the wrap-around porch. Many people were dabbing at their eyes, but none seemed to be as grief-stricken as I was. My eye spied across the lawn the casket: closed. The area around it had been adorned with pretty flowers. and a place for the preacher to stand had been established. My eyes grew hot again with tears.

Finally, we could see where a second set of steps descended into the lawn on one side, and two wide doors opened up into the house on the other side. I could see people slowly choosing between these two destinations. Some would disappear into the house while others would go and find their seats on the lawn. At the end of this line, I surmised, were Myrtle's remaining living relatives (though I recognized that perhaps everyone at the funeral was included in that category!) receiving their guests.

Then it was the turn of the people immediately in front of me, and they turned to explore the house. There, standing in front of me, in all of her glory, was Myrtle! Alive and well! Tom, Maxwell, and Samuel collectively lost their breath. From their perspective, I knew, she seemed just a couple of years older than they were, yet even Jessica and Sydney emitted an 'oooooooooh.' Myrtle was wearing a brilliantly white dress and showed no hint on her face of sorrow. Jessica caught her breath and said, very quietly, "She's the most beautiful thing I have ever seen."

Then I heard Myrtle say to my parents, "Please do find me before you leave. We have much to talk about regarding your son, Casey." Then, she winked at me, and my parents practically had to shove us all down the steps into the lawn area to find our seats.

Myrtle was not dead! Who was in the casket?

# Chapter 11

I suppose that the ceremony was beautiful and served its purpose, but I was transfixed, like so many others, by the presence of the living Myrtle seated not too far from the casket holding what everyone believed was the dead Myrtle. I was elated to know that she still lived. My grief had been chased away like a fox with hounds in fast pursuit. Yet, I wondered about the casket, and all of the people present for the funeral, and contemplated how it was that my own parents knew Myrtle. My parents, on the other hand, had been wondering how the last living relative of old Myrtle, the sparkling brand-new *new* Myrtle, knew of me. I guessed that they were trying to guess what she wanted to do with me, and while I was not surprised she wanted to see me again, I too wondered what she had in mind that qualified as 'much to talk about.'

Time slowed down. After the service, there was eating. After the eating, people lined up again to pay their respects to the new Myrtle. It was hours before the line of people dwindled enough that my parents thought it might be possible to actually have a conversation with her. At last we were standing before her. Her crystal blue eyes and joyous smile greeted us each in turn.

"I should like it if you could stay just for a while longer," Myrtle said. "Why don't you wait in the house? Help yourself to some tea and cakes. Casey, why don't you lead them—you know the way—while I have a word with your parents?"

My parents exchanged perplexed looks. I glanced at her uneasily, but she said again, "Go on, Casey. Take your brothers and sisters. Your parents will be right along."

Curiosity kept my head craning over my shoulder to try to hear what Myrtle was sharing with my parents, but a sense of pride turned my head back to the house as I noticed my brothers and sisters looking at me with new respect, mystified not only that the lady had an interest in our family and me in particular, but that I, who they knew confidently had never been here before, 'knew the way.'

Indeed, the moment I walked through the door it was clear that it was the same house. Forgetting that my siblings were with me, I circled the foyer, reaching every which way to try to put my hands on the Tree of Life which I knew must be rising up into the house. My hands fell on nothing more than empty air and things common to an ordinary house. I was disappointed, yet I knew in my bones that it *was* there.

A room off of the foyer had a large dining room table in the middle of it. Tea, cakes, and candies adorned the whole length of it. A sign at each end read, "Help yourself!" It looked like no one had touched any of it all day. Else, it had been replenished with them in mind. Despite my desire to know what was going on and a growing urge to sneak upstairs to see Myrtle's room once again, the chocolates defeated me. I joined my siblings at the table for the delectable feast that was set before us.

About five minutes later, my parents walked in. My father looked at me, shaking his head and smiling slightly. My mother didn't look at me at all. She wore a worried expression. Informing us that Myrtle would be along shortly, they sat down at the table and helped themselves to tea. When Myrtle hadn't come along shortly, they helped themselves to cake. They still had their perplexed looks on, but they studiously did not look at me. After everyone had had their fill, my mother motioned for me to join my father and her in one of the side rooms.

"Well, Casey," Dad began. "The young lady we met is Myrtle's only living granddaughter. Ironically, her name is Myrtle, too. It seems that Myrtle's will included a provision to take on a worthy candidate to become a gentleman scholar from among her many relatives. How she settled on you, I have no idea, but she did. Granddaughter Myrtle has invited you to come stay with her, and there receive the finest education that money can buy."

My mother interjected, "You know that we have always said that we were going to have to pull ourselves up by our own bootstraps as far as education goes. We haven't enough to send all of you to college, especially with the way tuitions keep going up and up, and have generally believed it possible to get a quality education anyway, if you worked hard enough. Still, money does make it easier."

It was my father's turn to interrupt, "You'll be sent away to a well-known academy that was founded by prominent members of our family, more than a hundred years ago. But we won't make you do it. It's sure to be loads of work, far beyond what we already put you through."

"It's totally up to you," Mom said, something in her voice suggesting that she was very torn, as if she hoped that I would decline the offer.

"When do I start?" I cried out in excitement.

"See, that's what I mean," Dad said, looking askance at my mother. "Why do I feel like there's more going on here?"

I had no way of answering that without having them deem me crazy, but fortunately Mom answered for me, "We'll chalk it up to the grace of God."

Dad shrugged his shoulders in surrender, "To answer your question, if you accept the offer, you'll come home with us tonight, and then in about a week someone will come and get you."

"Yes, definitely. I accept," I stated emphatically. Any chance to be in the presence of Myrtle again was to be embraced. Also, I knew in my heart that any education that involved Myrtle was sure to mean more adventure than reading or tedious work.

"Well, that settles it, then," Dad said.

Mom hugged me.

We went back into the dining room, where we found young Myrtle holding court with my siblings. Jessica and Sydney were laughing so hard that no sound was coming out of their mouths, and they were bent over in their chairs, quivering. My brothers, however, were laughing as though the joke had been at their expense, and I noted that Tom's cheeks were slightly red. Myrtle had no shame, it seemed, for she was perched on a chair at the end of the table, pantomiming something I could not guess without more contest. She was exulting in the mirth of the game.

When she saw us come in the room she sat down and apologized for impolitely dancing on her own chairs and expressed her hope that we had all had enough to eat. My father indicated that we had and then told her that they had just shared her offer with me, and that I had accepted.

"Wonderful," Myrtle beamed.

"Offer?" Tom asked quizzically, tilting his head in my direction.

"We will be sure to have someone pick Casey up next week," Myrtle assured my parents. "Thank you so much for staying late to talk to me. I know it has been a long day."

"It was just fine," Mom told her.

"We will keep you informed of our progress!" Myrtle said.

"Thank you," Dad replied. "Now, I think it is time for us to go home."

"Offer?" Tom asked again, but no one answered him.

We were soon at home where Tom received his explanation, and the family heard the news. I had the distinct sense that Tom resented not being chosen himself, but this waned a few days later when we learned that the 'deceased' Myrtle had left an inheritance check for the whole family, designating funds to be set aside for each member of the family, including the requirement that trust funds be set up to pay for the college tuition of each of my siblings. More funds were specifically allowable for the whole family, and I knew that my parents were relieved that they could now afford to make some desperately needed repairs around the house.

The day before I was to be picked up, Dad took me aside and said, "It's interesting that Myrtle left money for one person to buy the best education that can be bought, and selected you, all the while providing enough money in trust funds for the rest of your brothers and sisters to afford the same. Can you explain this to me?"

I told him that I couldn't. Perhaps it would have been truer to say that I shouldn't. At any rate, I didn't.

# Chapter 12

I expected to be driven out to the house again, and was looking forward to it immensely, but found instead that we were headed to New York City—some twenty hours away. True, I had always wanted to visit this famed city, but I had figured when I did I would enter through the airport, not the highway. My driver was a stern looking man who introduced himself as Mr. Chaffee. He had reinforced his stern look with stern warnings to listen to what he said and always stay within his sight. Myrtle, I was told, was waiting for me in New York.

To kill time I found myself doing a lot of napping. I made attempts to read some of my favorite books that I had brought along, and on occasion I found something interesting to look at, but this never lasted long. I usually just drifted off, the rhythm of the car rocking me to sleep, even against my will.

"Record time," Mr. Chaffee announced to me as we pulled into the driveway of a small brick house after nearly a full day of driving. "Nineteen hours and thirty-eight minutes. Record time."

"Where's the city?" I wanted to know.

"You're in it, young sir," he replied. "It is a big city."

"I had imagined some apartment in some high rise or something," I protested.

"You mean you *assumed*," he corrected me, "but no one ever said anything of the sort."

"Will I get to see downtown?" I inquired.

"You will get to see Miss Myrtle in under a minute, and that is far better."

There was no arguing with that.

Mr. Chaffee led the way to the front door, which he promptly opened and shoved me through. He stood at the door a moment, looking up and down the street for dangers I could not guess.

The place smelled like the 1970s. The foyer was large enough only for two people and six boots. Old, yellowed vinyl flooring showed numerous stains. A battered brown bi-fold closet door was open slightly, showing a coat wrapped in plastic hanging inside. To my left I saw the living room. Pea-green carpet held up a dusty, long coffee table and a flower-patterned couch. A television from the same era was on a table in the corner.

"This way," Mr. Chaffee told me, leading me down a hallway.

The hallway opened up into a cramped kitchen where Myrtle was sitting at a small table, reading the newspaper. I couldn't put my finger on it, but it seemed that everything that touched her was newer where it did, and grew progressively older when she moved away from it. The table where her hands were looked spanking brand new, but the other end the table looked like it was on its last legs.

"Casey!" Myrtle exclaimed, leaping up to greet me. She embraced me, but I was momentarily distracted by the fact that the brand new portion of the table now looked like its brother on the other side—decrepit, fading, and failing. No one can think of such things for long when being hugged by someone as alive as Myrtle, however, and I allowed myself to be wrapped up in her strong arms.

"Mr. Chaffee!" she shouted with as much joy as she had greeted me. She detached herself from me and now clung to him. He was taller by a head, so I could see his harsh features melt the moment she hugged him. After a moment, she let go of him, too, and the crudely cut angles of his face returned.

She returned to her seat and beckoned Mr. Chaffee and I to sit down. I noticed that her chair and the table where she touched it regained their fresh look. There was barely enough room at the table in that tight space, but we squeezed in, and she proceeded to pepper them with inquirers about the trip—what did we see, how was it, was it comfortable enough, and so on. I found myself answering in long rambling sentences that all ended in "and then I fell asleep," and Mr. Chaffee, in contrast, offered short, brief grunts and utterances in response to her questions.

As the evening wound down and I began to wonder precisely what Myrtle had in store for me, I asked her a question that was bugging me.

"Myrtle, why are we in this shack of a house when you could afford so much more? I thought we'd be in some high class apartment in a sky rise, overlooking the city!" I asked.

"Now, Casey," she said. "Don't you know by now that sometimes things are more than they appear? In fact, I will go so far as to say that they are *always* more than they appear. You are sitting in the oldest surviving structure in the New World." Seeing my disbelief, she added, "I trust that you know enough by now to believe me, whatever I have to say."

"Yes, Myrtle. I'm sorry. I didn't mean to suggest I didn't. It's just... the carpet... well, it's..." I stammered.

"Not very pretty?" she laughed. "Isn't it wonderful?"

Not noticing (or not caring) that I didn't at all understand, she continued on, "You will likely have a chance to witness all sorts of exotic things before we are done."

"And what are we doing?"

"Advancing your education, of course," she smiled.

"What shall I be learning?"

"Oh, so many things!" she laughed, then, looking askance to Mr. Chaffee, she said, "I suppose we may need to just come out and tell him."

Mr. Chaffee nodded, "It is only right. He accepted your offer, and you sold it to his parents, without indicating how dangerous it would be."

Myrtle grew quiet for a moment, wondering, I supposed, where to begin. As for me, my curiosity was well piqued. As for there being danger, I had figured that danger was part and parcel with adventure and was frankly counting on it. Myrtle had settled on a starting place.

"Dear Casey, haven't you wondered how it is that the Tree of Life came to be growing up in the middle of a house in the Midwest?" she asked me.

Well, that pulled me up short. I was shocked that the question hadn't presented itself to my mind, before. What did I know about the Tree of Life prior to meeting Myrtle? I knew that according to the old story, it was originally planted in the Garden of Eden. No one knew where this was located anymore. It was destroyed during the Great Deluge, and though I had never thought about it before, presumably the Tree of Life had been destroyed along with it. Myrtle was quite right: how was it that the Tree of Life still existed, and how did it come to be planted in a continent far, far away?

I admitted, "I hadn't previously thought about it, but now that you mentioned it, it *is* mighty curious."

"Well, I think we need to start with that before we can talk about the rest," she said. "However, I don't think we can have that conversation until we've had some food. There is a fine pizza place in the area that delivers. How would you like some authentic New York pizza?"

"That would be great!" I exclaimed. I was hungry. I was tired, too. It had been many hours in a vehicle, but adrenalin and anticipation was driving me now.

"Very well. I will make the call. While I do that, Mr. Chaffee will take you and your belongings upstairs to your room. Settle in a bit, and I'll call you down when the food is here," she instructed.

Mr. Chaffee grabbed my bags. I scooped up what was left, and followed him up some rickety old steps. I saw on the walls in the staircase numerous paintings and some occasional old black and white photographs. In some of them, I recognized the old Myrtle. That made me wonder why the great charade to fake her death. I would ask her the next time I thought of it, I told myself.

Finding my bedroom, I opened up my suitcase, sat on my bed, and promptly fell asleep.

# Chapter 13

I awoke to the sounds of laughter downstairs. It was darker outside than when I first went upstairs, and I wondered if it was morning or evening. A hunger pang shot through me, and it was followed closely by a pang of disappointment that I didn't get to enjoy some freshly cooked authentic New York pizza! I put myself together in the bathroom and sauntered down the stairs to see what was going on. Myrtle and Mr. Chaffee were in the kitchen. Before I stepped out of the hallway into the kitchen, the two were laughing uproariously, but the moment my eyes landed on Mr. Chaffee, his face became grim. Myrtle seemed not to notice, and greeted me warmly.

"See, Casey. You haven't been sleeping long. Mr. Chaffee guessed that you would fall asleep, so we decided to wait until you woke up before ordering the pizza. Let me make that call now," she said.

As she was placing the order on the phone, I sat across from Mr. Chaffee wondering what it was that had him laughing so hard a moment earlier, and why when I had entered the room he had tightened up so rapidly. Perhaps he didn't like me.

"That pizza will be here in under thirty minutes, I wager," Myrtle informed me, sitting down in her place.

"I hope you got enough! I could eat three whole pizzas myself, I bet!" I said.

"That's why I got four," she giggled.

Mr. Chaffee set a tall glass of pop in front of me, and after a few other pleasantries, Myrtle began telling her story.

"It is called Bulgaria now, but at that time it had no name and indeed wasn't a country at all..."

### ***

Myrtle gazed out of her window, watching her three children play in the yard. Her hands were busy, grinding grains of wheat into flour. Her mind was on the vegetables and the dwindling stores of fruit on her shelves. She mopped some of the sweat off of her brow; it was hot on account of the fire being stoked to bake some bread. Despite the momentary discomfort, watching her children running around and her husband out chopping wood, she was content. It had been ten years of a good life together. True, there had been times of scarcity and hardship, and never any times of bounty, but in her estimation, they'd always had enough.

And now they had enough flour. She put the rest of the wheat away. The bread was done, so she pulled that out of the oven and set it on the table to cool. She grabbed one of her fruit jars and frowned at how light it was. She looked inside. There were only a few berries left, and for a family of five, they wouldn't last another meal. It was nigh time for that meal, so she put the matter out of her mind for a few moments and set the table.

Soon, her husband came in, the children tumbling after.

Once supper was fully in progress, Myrtle brought up the matter of the fruit.

"Tomorrow I will go up the mountain to replenish our jars with berries," she told her husband.

"You'll take the eldest with you?" he asked.

"As usual," she replied.

"I should think that you could collect enough to last a little longer," he remarked.

"With the way you all eat? I don't think so," she smiled.

"Someday we will be able to hire a servant or two, and then you will be able to carry more," her husband said, switching his attention to their oldest son. "And soon enough, you'll be strong enough to carry quite a bit, too!" He rubbed his son's hair, which was already so wild it looked no different after being tussled.

"*Dad...*"

"Actually, I would like to leave him. I'll be home much sooner that way," Myrtle replied. "What he can carry doesn't quite make up for the fact that he doesn't... move that fast."

This was all true, but the whole truth was that Myrtle wanted some time alone. She loved her family but all the more when she hadn't seen them for a few hours. There was another reason: she had a secret place where she liked to go. It was hard to get there, requiring a difficult trek up the mountain, through thickets, into a canyon, and over a creek, but it was well worth the efforts. It was her secret grove. She had found it when she herself had been young and had never told a soul about it. There was also a multitude of berries of different kinds there, which justified the trip. When her family went berry collecting with her, she went elsewhere.

The next morning, she woke early. After setting out food for breakfast, she stowed a bit of bread for herself, and threw a sack of empty jars over her shoulders. She knew that she would regret having to carry them all back, full, but she knew her husband would like having a stocked kitchen. She didn't mind it, either.

She journeyed up the misty mountain for about an hour, after which the sun was high enough in the sky to cook off the rest of the fog. Knowing she was about halfway to her destination, she decided to take a short break to eat some of her bread. She sat down on a large boulder and enjoyed the scenery.

It was then that she heard it.

She reached for her knife, only to discover that she had forgotten it. Fighting a bear was never one's first option, but at least having a weapon gave her the option, which was better than not having it at all. Without even that possibility, she knew she'd be left with flight, and she'd have to leave her jars and abandon her mission. The bear was standing in her path to her secret grove, anyway. No doubt, it had been attracted by the scent of her food.

"Go away, bear!" she tried shouting.

It stood up on its hind legs and answered with a deafening roar.

Myrtle laughed, which was good, because Casey was starting to get nervous about where the story was going. She said, "That was a *mean* bear."

Myrtle quickly took stock of her situation and realized that she could not get by the bear and that it would be unwise to try fleeing down the path. She made a motion as to go to the left, which the bear matched, indicating to her that the bear meant to attack her no matter what. She quickly fished out a smaller jar and threw it at the bear's head. This she realized had not been wise, either, as that seemed to enrage it further. Myrtle yelped, threw the remaining half of her loaf of bread at the bear, and fled up the mountain.

She ran and ran and ran until she could run no more. The bear was nowhere to be seen, but she quickly determined that she was lost. She had a sense of the way she had come, but didn't dare to go back that way. The bear had probably followed her a bit. How far, she didn't know. But where was she now? For as often as she'd come up the mountain in this direction, she'd always made straight for her hidden grove. She was in unexplored territory.

Once she caught her breath, she wandered around a bit, studiously avoiding the route she had taken to get there to make sure she didn't stumble upon the thing that had driven her that way in the first place. Myrtle looked for another way down the mountain, and home, but every direction she went seemed to have obstacles. They could be overcome if she really needed to, but she preferred a less treacherous path if she could find one, so she continued to probe her surroundings, looking for the path of least resistance.

This she didn't find, but she did find some of her favorite berries. Famished, she ate all the ones she could see. Then, she caught the smell of something really delectable, and just like that bear chasing the scent of bread, she followed the aroma wherever it led. It was not an easy journey. At one point she had to leap across a deep crevice—fortunately, it was narrow, but she couldn't see the bottom of it—and in another place she had to scale a ten-foot high rock face. That was no easy task, but the smell drove her on.

Suddenly, she found the source of the aroma. She stood in a clearing that was carved into the mountain and beheld a tall, magnificent tree standing in the middle of it. Soft grass covered the area around it, which was bounded by rock walls on all but the side she had entered. Her berry plants adorned the edges, but she had only eyes for the tree.

Large, translucent fruits hung from the branches. She found it odd that she could smell the tree. It was normal to smell the blossoms of fruit trees, but once the blossoms had turned to fruit, their scent disappeared, or at least diminished. Not so, in this case. The scent was overwhelming, even pungent, at this close distance, but the fruits hung heavy regardless.

Myrtle circled the tree cautiously. You cannot know how strong the desire she had to reach out, take and eat! However, wisdom had taught her to be cautious about what one ingested. A completely new fruit could as easily be poisonous as healthy, and she knew that performing the necessary experiment so far from home could spell her doom. But, oh, she wanted to! If she were not already stuffed on berries, who knows what she would have done...

Instead, she carefully plucked a dozen of them and stowed them safely in her garments. It was time to descend down the mountain... bear, or no bear. She carefully made note of her path, and eventually found her way back into familiar territory. She would retrieve her jars some other time. She made right for home, instead.

Myrtle's husband knew something was amiss immediately and met her at the door.

"You have to see what I have!" she exclaimed, going right to the kitchen table and laying out the fruits.

"What are they? Where did you get them?" he asked.

"From a tree that I found on the mountain!" she replied.

He hunched over them, putting his nose right up to them in a close inspection, "They smell wonderful. Did you eat one?"

"No, of course not."

"Someone will have to try them. If they taste as good as they smell, it might be worth dying just to eat them," he said.

"Let's give a bit to the dog," Myrtle suggested.

Her husband quickly concurred, and fetched the animal. He set a bit on the floor and the dog wasted no time devouring it, and then looking about for more. They watched it for awhile to see if it would die, or fall ill. It merely whined for more.

"If only we had a slave, we could make him try it," he said. "Another time it would be useful to be rich."

"Perhaps we have some prisoners?"

"No. I would know," he replied. "I am going to get the chief and the elders to inspect it, and then I will try it myself if there are no others. Keep the children away."

He left and speedily returned with the village chief and a half dozen elders. They also thought it looked and smelled wonderful, adding that something that smelled so nice and looked so precious could not possibly be poisonous.

"Just to be safe," Myrtle's husband said, "I'll go first in trying it."

He nibbled around the tip... "Exquisite!"

That was all the permission anyone needed. Everyone present grabbed one and devoured it. The word 'exquisite' didn't do it justice. It was beyond wonderful.

Myrtle thought aloud, "How to describe it... sweet, yes. Sweet like a strawberry, but not a hint of the tartness of a strawberry."

"Almost like sweet, juicy bread," said the chief.

"If beer were a fruit, this would be what it would taste like," said one of the elders.

"Too sweet," Myrtle's husband countered. "No bitterness at all; definitely a fruit."

The chief put his hand out on the chair as though he had been suddenly wracked with pain, except his face looked peaceful. The worry-wrinkles on his face seem to melt away and a healthy pink hue filled his cheeks.

"Chief, are you OK?" Myrtle reached out to him.

She was interrupted as the elders likewise fell into a spasm. Their gray hair fell out of their heads and was replaced by the hair color they had as youths; indeed, their bodies contorted in order to match what was happening on on top of their heads.

"I saw this happen to you!" Casey said.

"Then I know exactly what you saw," Myrtle replied.

Soon, the bodies of the chiefs and the elders were fully transformed into those of strapping young men. Myrtle supposed that she did not undergo that kind of radical change because she was only twenty-five, anyway, and her husband likewise relatively young, but even she found upon inspection of her body that a wart she had only just discovered had completely disappeared.

"Where did you find this fruit?" the chief asked.

Myrtle saw a dark cloud come over her husband's demeanor.

# Chapter 14

It did not take very long before word spread. The wives of the elders were the first to come to Myrtle's house, they being old and walking with careful, deliberate footsteps, and their strapping young husbands helping them along by lending them their arms. Myrtle came out to greet them, a wide smile on her face.

"Isn't it wonderful? They are young and healthy!" she exclaimed with joy.

"But I am still old and withered," shot back the one closest to her.

"How dare you heal my husband and not me!" shouted another.

Myrtle's smile vanished as the old women began to assail her with complaints. She stepped backwards into her doorway as if to keep danger in front of her rather than on all sides. "We can heal you, too! I only brought enough for a handful, but there is enough for a town of two hundred, easily!" Myrtle told them. "I'll be happy to go back and bring more, assuming I can find it again." She felt a tug on her elbow, and then a yank, and suddenly she was inside her house and the door was closed shut. The old women continued to throw complaints at her through the door, but it was her husband that now had her attention.

"Something like this, people would pay generously for," he said. "As finders of the tree, our family deserves its just reward. Let us go back to the tree, but secretly, and return with enough to make everyone happy, and ourselves rich."

"Rich?" Myrtle asked.

"They will pay handsomely for this, I assure you. Now, go out there and tell them that you will indeed acquire more of the fruit, and they should think carefully about what they are willing to pay for it," he ordered her.

"They are our friends and family! Let them share in our joy!" Myrtle protested.

"I have every intention of doing just that—but for a price. Now, go. Tell them," he said, opening the door and pushing her out to fulfill his command. She was embarrassed to have to say such things to those who were so close to her, but to her surprise, the old women did not offer any retort.

"We will be here and ready when you come back," they said.

Early the next morning, Myrtle's husband gathered up the entire family and prepared them for the journey. Myrtle tried her best to explain where they would have to go so that they would be up for the task. Each child carried baskets. Her husband strapped on a sword—to deal with the bear, he said, but Myrtle knew better. He was concerned about the others in the village. This became obvious when Myrtle suggested that they leave the kids behind so that they could go faster, but he insisted that this would be a bad idea, because they may be kidnapped while they were gone and held hostage for the fruit.

"These are our friends and family!" Myrtle had protested.

"We will see soon enough how far that goes," he had replied, ending the discussion.

Her husband had been more right than wrong. Even before they left the town there were people trying to follow them. They made a handful of half-measured attempts to evade the ones following them, but finally her husband became exasperated and told them in no uncertain terms that they would not go get any fruit at all if people persisted in trying to track them. He made good on his threat by finally turning the family around and going back home. After that, the townsfolk relented, and did not follow them. That does not mean that they did not resent this treatment bitterly. Myrtle could tell by the looks on their faces that they would never forgive them for this.

Myrtle first went to the place where the bear had surprised her. It was not hard to recognize, for it had been on a part of the mountain she was familiar with, and besides, her jars were still there where she had dropped them. The bear, thankfully, was nowhere to be seen.

It was not hard to figure out the general direction she had fled, but after just twenty minutes or so she could no longer recognize where she was or what her next steps were. She wandered around the mountain side, towing her family around, trying to ignore the glowering look her husband was giving her. He nearly exploded in anger when they had found their way back to the same spot for a third time. It was then that Myrtle caught the scent.

"This way!" she shouted.

Though it proved to be even longer than she remembered, she knew she was on the right track when she found the narrow, bottomless fissure that she had leapt over, and the aroma became increasingly noticeable. The geography became more recognizable, as if enhanced by the strong association with the smell of the tree. Her turns became more direct and more efficient, confirmed by discernible changes in the strength of the scent.

Then, it was as though the scent was a tidal wave washing over them, drowning them, and overpowering them; they were in the clearing. There, nestled in an indentation of the mountain, bounded on three sides with tall, rocky walls, was the tree. Its white fruit sparkled despite the fact that the sunlight just barely invaded the space. The wide green leaves beckoned them, and they obeyed.

It was strange, though. Myrtle did not want another bite. Neither, apparently, did her husband. Their children could barely be restrained, but once they had eaten, they too fell indifferent to the fruit. Instead, they seemed to be drawn to the tree itself. The children found a way into the branches and ascended as high as they could, frolicking, as well as one could on tree limbs. Myrtle, however, was overcome with the impression that they were not alone, that they were not entirely welcome, that they had trespassed on the nearest thing to the sacred that she'd ever experienced.

Her husband—not so much.

He quickly set himself to the task of harvesting the fruit and chastised Myrtle for not helping him with the same kind of enthusiasm that he had for the job. It did not take too long for the job to be done, however, because even though the baskets they had brought were not even a third of the way full, they were much heavier than Myrtle recalled. Too many more of them in the baskets, and they would not be able to be carried at all. Finally, he relented and summoned them for the trip back. Myrtle had not mentally marked the way to or from the tree with any great care, but her husband rectified that.

He was also very deliberate in circling around their home and arriving from a direction that people would not expect, and he was wise to do so, because they were spotted at once, and, giving them a wide birth, men dove into the woods in an attempt to retrace their path. However, no one expected the welcome they would receive once they actually arrived at their house.

It was not just the occupants of their own town that were waiting for them, but also people from the towns nearest, as well. There would not be enough fruit for all who showed up. Myrtle could tell that her husband couldn't decide if this was a good thing, or a bad thing.

"You all know why you are here!" he shouted over the din of the thousand or more people who had gathered. "I see that many of you have brought gold, silver, and other items to trade for this fruit. We shall have bidding, because I do not have enough for everyone. Someone will have to go without. The ones with the highest offers will be the ones who receive the fruit."

At this, the great crowd responded with a mixture of pleasure and anger. There was cursing and jostling, and Myrtle was suddenly afraid for her life. The people began pressing in on them, and then, suddenly they were not: her husband had drawn his sword and thrust it into the stomach of a man who had drawn too close. The crowd drew back in startled fear and amazement.

"I *will* kill any who try to take that which is mine to give. You may overpower me, and some of you may get the fruit, but once it is gone, know this—I am the only one who knows the way back. If you all want some, then I will happily return and get some more. Maybe I should have said that *today*, someone will have to go without. If you can be just a little patient, and do not blather on to all of the people in nearby cities, by this time tomorrow, or maybe the day after, you *all* can enjoy new life!" her husband announced.

In the main, this seemed to satisfy them, but there were still some angry outbursts.

"Caudry the Wealthy is here and can outbid us all, including your kinsmen," said one of his own townsfolk. "It is only right that you should serve the ones whom you actually will have to live with for the rest of your life!" Caudry the Wealthy was the name of a man of great wealth who lived in the town next to theirs. Myrtle's husband shrewdly detected both the threat in his kinsmen's words but also the opportunity—he would need people loyal to him to preserve his own life.

But he also remembered that once he had returned to the tree, he had no more interest in the fruit. It was not something that people would want to come back for, over and over again. He would have to exact a cost from people right from the beginning, because otherwise there would not be another chance.

"Very well!" he said. "I will make a compromise! I will serve my own townspeople first, but there will still be bidding, and there will be a minimum cost. If you cannot afford this minimum, then you must be prepared to pay what you have left. Also, you must eat the fruit immediately, in my presence. I will not have anyone trying to sneak off and plant the fruit instead, and so acquire their own tree. I will *kill* anyone who tries. Is it all agreed?"

Now there was universal agreement, and the bidding began.

Myrtle's husband extracted a high cost, indeed. The first person to win was the chief himself, who turned over the rule of the town to him and after that almost his entire manor, reserving for himself just a handful of slaves and a small house. The chief himself had already eaten of the fruit, and knew its worth firsthand, but his wife was still decrepit. Love drove him to give up nearly everything for her. Once she too ate the fruit in the presence of the assembly and underwent the great transformation, there were no more skeptics left; if anyone could have bid more than the chief himself had, they surely would have done so. As it is, many of them gave as much as they had, retaining nothing.

Finally, there reached a point where the people could offer nothing that could compel him to give up the fruit. These were primarily young men who had not yet had time in life to acquire possessions or security.

"Dear brother," they cried out to him, "why should we be

penalized for our youth? We would give it all if only we had it! Why should strangers from around and about have this great gift and not us, your own relatives! Surely we have something, by virtue of our blood-relation, to offer!"

He had perhaps anticipated this all along, because he was ready.

Before he could answer them, though, there was a commotion. At the end of the last sale, the man tried to deceive them all into thinking he had eaten it, but he was caught and dragged forward. It was one of Myrtle's cousins, but there was no mercy granted: her husband stepped forward and slew him on the spot.

"Do you wish to offer me anything?" he shouted, climbing on top of a nearby rock. "Then give me the thing you value the most—your very life. Swear to me that you will be mine and will be my servant, and I will serve you with *new* life. Swear to me!"

At this, many of the young men recoiled. They were not so old as to feel they needed the fruit as much as their fathers and grandfathers. Only about ten of them stepped forward to accept the terms of the offer, and these were those who were born with deformities, or were sickly, or had been crippled by accidents early on in their lives.

As each of the ten ate the fruit, he gave them one of the new swords he had acquired and then their first orders: to protect him and his family. To the death.

Having nothing else to do, and of course being immensely grateful for being healed in dramatic fashion, they complied.

Overnight, Myrtle's husband had become chief and warlord and rich beyond his dreams. He was happier than he had ever been. Myrtle, however, was deeply unsettled, and did not know why.

# Chapter 15

Myrtle had allowed her eyes to focus on the wall beside me as she told her story. I had long stopped eating my pizza. A heavy silence had fallen upon the room. Her eyes drifted away from the wall until they met mine, and bespying the tell-tale moisture in them that I knew were the precursor of tears, I felt my heart breaking again. Someone as innocent and beautiful as the young Myrtle in pain was enough to crack open the earth itself, something I knew in my gut to be a fact, as true and real as anything I believed was true and real.

Finally, she spoke again.

"The next year, we went back to the tree—ourselves and the tree protected now by a small army—but there were no fruit to be found on it. This generated great disappointment, much resentment, and eventually bloodshed, for many in the region who had not partaken the previous year had gathered to eat the next year. All in all, in my view, it had been a bitter-sweet experience.

"We returned regularly for many years after that without ever finding another harvest. In my view, even at the time, that was to the good. Already those who had eaten of the fruit had taken their new youth and vigor to mischievous and often deadly ends. It grew worse after several decades had gone by and those who had eaten the fruit didn't appear to age. After seventy or eighty years, it became clear that death of old age was not forthcoming. Furthermore, many people who had sustained injuries over those years had shown rapid, miraculous healing. Only one of them had died in all that time, and it had been a most terrible experience. He had committed a horrible crime, one eminently deserving death, but when it came time to carry out the sentence, no matter what horrid measure they employed, he would not die. Eventually they had to... well... I will not speak of it."

Myrtle shuddered at the thought.

"Well, after about a hundred years had gone by and we hadn't aged a day, we became interested in an explanation. You see, the tree hadn't yielded another harvest in all that time, and many of us had had many, many more children. These children were abnormally healthy and thrived. You should remember that times were different then, and many people died in their childhood. The children of those who ate the fruit lived much longer than those born at the same time from parents who had not eaten of the fruit, but at last even they began to grow old and die. Not one of them lived beyond one hundred and twenty years. There were many who wanted fruit made available for their children and grandchildren and great-grandchildren, but none could be produced. They knew well enough that if it could be, my husband, knowing what kinds of riches it would mean for him, would have made it available. Still, even I knew the heartache of losing loved ones. It is often said that one should not outlive their own children. Well, I was outliving my own grandchildren. Between the two sentiments—concern for one's own kin and the desire to harvest another crop—my husband and I began searching for information that could help us understand this tree.

"That brought us to Karanovo, a city that was ancient even in our own day, although at that time it did not have that name. In Karanovo, we found only one person who could help us, a Jew known as Jakov."

With that, Myrtle fell once again into the depths of her memories.

Myrtle had been regarded as a queen in her own town, but Karanovo dwarfed her city in size and importance. Even so, their entourage was met by crowds of curious people. It was disquieting to realize that these people had heard about them from their long deceased grandparents and great-grandparents. As far as the people of Karanovo were concerned, Myrtle and her family, and all those who had eaten the fruit, were legends. At least, that was the case until they entered the town with their great company of servants, soldiers, hired merchants, and the like.

The king of Karanovo came and greeted them and invited them to stay with him in his residence, but Myrtle's husband was much more comfortable sleeping in the fields, surrounded by his own people. He did, however, quietly make inquiries. The king was asked about the wise men of the town, and which, if any, might know anything about trees with miraculous powers.

The king shared a knowing smile, and vowed to do his best.

Several days later, a messenger arrived. Scrawled on a piece of pottery was the word Jakov and underneath that, the phrase, Dung Street.

The next morning, Myrtle and her husband discretely left their camp on the outskirts of Karanovo, hiding among their own merchants as the merchants went into the center of the city to carry out their trade. Having arrived in the busy square, teeming with people doing business, they began searching for Dung Street. It was not difficult to find; one merely followed the smell. And Jakov was not difficult to find, either. His name was carved into a very large board that was far bigger than any of the other boards advertising wares.

"In here," Myrtle's husband said, pulling her into Jakov's shop.

"May I help you?" asked Jakov.

Jakov was a very, very old man. He had actually probably been alive when Myrtle had first eaten of the fruit. He sat at a table in a corner of the main room. Throughout the room were various other tables, all of them filled with heaping piles of plates made of metal and stone and other instruments for eating and cooking, such as metal pots.

"We were told that you might be able to tell us something about trees with life-giving powers," Myrtle's husband said.

The man looked at them and regarded them impassively. He looked at them so long that eventually Myrtle was worried he had died. "Sir?" Myrtle prodded him.

"So, these are the two who are the source of so many legends," Jakov said.

"They are mostly true, as you can see plainly," Myrtle's husband replied.

"I see," Jakov said. Then Jakov was quiet again, until finally Myrtle's husband took a turn prodding him.

"Why were we told that you might be able to help us?" he asked Jakov.

"My people are known as the Jews. We can trace our days to the very beginning of things, and have kept our history current. In our history, we know of a tree such as the one that legend

72

says you have partaken of; of course, I doubt very much that it was the same tree, for that would not make any sense at all, since it is certain that it was destroyed," Jakov said.

"Where was this tree?" Myrtle's husband asked.

"Very far from here. My people were driven out from our land by the Assyrians, but my father came here before that happened. Prophecies had been made about our impending destruction, and my father was among the few who believed. We left in time to bring with us much of our wealth, and we were able to establish ourselves here. Our countrymen were not so fortunate; they were scattered to the four winds, and I don't think any of them can be found today," Jakov said.

"What does that have to do with the tree?" he asked.

Jakov held up his hands, palms outward, as if to deflect a blow. "The one thing that we did not have were the writings of our people. However, my father committed much of it to memory, and I in turn have done the same. In our memory, we know of a tree that gave life, but we also know that our ancestors were forbidden from eating of it. So you see, you could not eat of this tree. Even if it were not now destroyed, you would have been prevented from eating of it."

"I will gladly pay to have a scribe write down this story, so that I may take it with me," Myrtle's husband said.

"How is that to my benefit?" Jakov replied.

Irritated, Myrtle's husband replied, "Very well, I shall hire two scribes to record your story, and you may have one of the copies. This assumes, of course, that what you have to tell me is helpful."

Jakov studied them carefully. He clearly welcomed the prospect of having a written copy of his memories. Myrtle wondered if it might be because there was no son for Jakov to compel to memorize the stories that Jakov had engraved in his own mind. Perhaps Jakov feared that upon his death, the knowledge would be lost to the ages. At any rate, Jakov finally nodded and said, "It is agreed."

"Very well, then. Why don't you start with telling me why the tree you are thinking of was destroyed?" Myrtle's husband pressed Jakov.

Jakov sighed, "I fear that if I told you this history, you would consider it a fable, just as the people of this town have considered your existence to be a fable."

"Yet, I know that I am not a fable, so I will listen carefully to what you have to say," Myrtle's husband replied.

"Very well, then. The tree in question was no doubt destroyed in what we might call the Great Deluge. It was a great flood that destroyed all living things on this planet except for a small family that our God declared was righteous. The patriarch of this family was known as Noah. He is my own ancestor. Until the day of this flood, there was on the earth a magnificent garden. It was this garden that was meant originally to be our habitation, and it was occupied for a time by my first father, Adam. But the world was wicked, so God destroyed it—and the garden, and with it, no doubt, that which we call the Tree of Life," Jakov said. "Unless!" Jakov suddenly shouted, his face dramatically transforming, as though the mere thinking of the thought had given him new life.

"Unless what?" Myrtle asked.

"Why, as you can plainly see, the earth is once again filled with vegetation. All the trees and bushes and grasses would have had their seeds scattered throughout the waters. Perhaps they survived on great floating masses, or maybe in the mud that was left at the top of the mountains, but if these survived, then why not the seeds from the Tree of Life and the Tree of Knowledge of Good and Evil?" Jakov exclaimed.

Myrtle now looked upon me hard, pulling me hard from my attempts to imagine the way the world was a thousand years earlier.

"So," said Myrtle, "I said to Jakov, 'Are we to believe that the old stories of a great flood are actually true?' In return, he scoffed at me, and said, 'Am I to believe that you ate of a tree that has allowed you to stand before me, nearly two hundred years old, when you appear to not be a day over thirty?'

"I turned to my husband at that point and asked him, 'What do you think? Might there have really been a great flood and, before that, a garden where some powerful being planted a tree of life? Does that sound as impossible to you as it does to me?' But he was not looking at me. He was staring hard at the Jew. And do you know what my husband said then?" Myrtle asked, looking hard at me.

Realizing the question was not rhetorical, I ventured, "Did he say, 'Just because a story is very old doesn't mean it isn't very true?'"

She beamed at me, "See, you *are* special. No, that is *not* what he said. Without taking his eyes off that man or even blinking, my husband said, 'A Tree of Knowledge of Good and Evil, you say?'"

# Chapter 16

I sucked air into my lungs, realizing now that there were many other things that were likely to be true if in fact there existed—really—a Tree of Life. It followed as a matter of course that there would also be a Tree of Knowledge of Good and Evil. What else might be true that hadn't yet registered in my mind?

"Did—did he find it?" I asked Myrtle, noting that Mr. Chaffee grimaced at the thought.

"Indeed, he did. The Jewish gentleman realized his error right away and pleaded with my husband not to go looking for this tree. I also begged him. The Jew reminded us that, according to the story, while there had not been any prohibition from eating of the Tree of Life, there *was* one against eating of the Tree of Knowledge of Good and Evil. In fact, the first humans were cast out of the garden after they had eaten from this forbidden tree, just so that they could not reach out, take, and eat of the Tree of Life, and so live forever. What devastating consequences had followed from eating of the Tree of Knowledge of Good and Evil! What would be the result if it was eaten of again, and this time from someone who had eaten of the Tree of Life? But he found it. And he ate of it."

"Wow," I exhaled. "What happened?"

"Many horrible things. However, you should understand that I was not there for that. He soon sent me back home and then he disappeared for a long while. I would hear rumors and stories, but he lost interest in me and his family until long after the Greeks had conquered our homeland. You see, as it turned out, while eating of the Tree of Life did give you immortality, one progressively lost one's vigor as time went on. If you did not eat again of the Tree of Life… well… you saw what happened to me. It was happening to me then, just as it was happening to him. He turned up again a little under seven hundred years after we had first eaten of the fruit. I knew of it, but concealed myself from him. He went and ate, and then later on I did as well. When he was gone again, I took the remaining fruit and distributed it to those who were left, and then I took an axe to the tree," Myrtle said sadly.

"You cut it down?" I was aghast.

"Dear Casey, you don't know the trouble it meant to live on and on and on while others around you were dying after three generations. It got worse as time went on. You couldn't tell people about it anymore. They'd destroy you as a witch, or something like that. One had to go about constantly faking one's death, or moving to an area where you were not known. When death was inflicted, it was a horrible, horrible death, as I alluded to earlier."

"Wow. Just *wow*," I breathed.

Myrtle took on a reminiscent air, and staring out into deep space, added, "Yes, I do believe they are all dead now. All that remains is me... and my husband."

Mr. Chaffee squeezed her hand, and a gentle smile chased away the sad look that had cropped up on her beautiful face. "It will be over some day," he comforted her.

"Indeed," she replied.

"So, an immortal can still be killed? How does that work?" I asked, perhaps a little too directly. Myrtle had shied away twice from giving details. There was probably a good reason for it.

"Well, just think of it this way—if someone is incinerated, for example, what then? Are their ashes still alive?" she responded.

"Is that then basically what happened to them all?" I brazenly ventured on. I felt that I had to know. It wasn't (purely) morbid curiosity. I was concerned too about Myrtle's eventual fate.

She deliberated carefully on her words, "You may guess that if one's body is completely un-constituted, it will take God himself to restore you. But a fair many were incinerated. That was the fate of the noble three-hundred that died at Thermopylae. Yes, a great many of the immortals ended up serving as mercenaries, and you can well imagine why. Many of these eventually settled in Sparta in Greece. It took thousands of Persians to put them down, finally, and 'un-constitute' them. But, please, let's not speak of this aspect any further."

"Yes, I'm sorry, Myrtle," I lowered my eyes.

Mr. Chaffee interjected, "But now you need to tell him the rest."

I looked up again, and saw that the sadness had crept back into her features.

"You're right, of course," Myrtle replied.

"I'm ready," I told her.

"Of course you are," she smiled kindly at me. "Allow me to continue."

***

Myrtle lay awake, reflecting on what she had done. The scent of the Tree of Life had overwhelmed her the moment she put her axe to it. The tree seemed sad, yet resigned, as though it understood what must be done; or else, something so precious and filled with joy is unable to have its joy extinguished, right up to the end. She set it all on fire. When she went back to town, everyone knew what she had done because the glorious smell had spread for miles and miles around. They looked at her sadly, without any joy.

But she suddenly had a thought.

"Perhaps there had been more than the one seed that survived the flood?"

The thought horrified her. Based on what she had learned from the Jew at Karanovo and some rough calculations, she guessed that the tree only bore fruit every seven hundred years. She had already come to grips with the fact that she would likely be alive after another seven hundred years had passed, so, frightened about what would happen if humanity at large discovered another tree, she made up her mind to seek out any other trees... and destroy them.

Then, she slept in peace.

Over the next few months, she made her plans quietly and without haste, but then word came that her husband had returned to the area for another batch of the fruit. For some reason, she never took into account the fact that her husband would come back. The implications struck her immediately once she did give this fact its proper weight. He was a changed man; wife, or no wife, he would strike her down. She gathered up everything she could carry in a couple of bags and fled her home and village, doubting she'd ever return.

The news eventually tracked her down and informed her that

her husband had indeed been outraged and vowed to murder her the moment he caught up with her. The news found her, but her husband did not. Myrtle was an intelligent woman to begin with. The fruit of the Tree of Life had strengthened her mind along with her body. She knew how to do the things necessary to remain hidden, even as she carried out her quest.

A side effect of having a healthy life that persisted so long, is that it makes it possible, with careful thought, hard work, and discernment, to acquire wealth, skill, and the wisdom normally associated only with the elderly. She started out destitute, but after a hundred and fifty years she had established herself as a great lady in several parts of the world, and with her sizable estates, purchased influence, protection, and discretion. Once she felt that her affairs were in order, she began her search for the remaining Trees of Life.

When one takes old tales seriously, rather than discounting them out of hand, one is able to accomplish great things, especially if your business concerns those old tales. In the wilds of Africa she heard stories about a tree of youth surrounded by a very protective tribe of fierce warriors. It took years, but she was able to eventually infiltrate the area, locate the tree, and destroy it. She fled without being discovered, but just because she paid no price didn't mean that no one did. The warrior tribe slaughtered their neighbors until there were no more, thinking that one of the nearby tribes was responsible. Myrtle wept when she learned of it.

Another story took her to Asia, where there was an old legend of an oasis in the middle of the desert. She found the tree untended and unguarded, and destroyed it forthwith. She was sad to have to destroy something as wonderful as a Tree of Life, but she was glad that this time no people would die because of it. The nagging realization that no people would live more fully because of her deed kept her from being too satisfied.

It was fitting that it was Asia, where she had this realization, that she began to bleed, although she eventually concluded that she had actually contracted the disease whilst in Africa, where she had observed others suffering similarly.

Myrtle remembered what it had been like to get sick, but she had not known illness for centuries by this point, except vicariously through others. She was shocked, therefore, when every morning her sheets would be covered with blood. Every morning for a year.

No doubt, she had come across some infection that even the powers of the Tree of Life could not wholly thwart. Even so, while she would be weak in the morning, the power of the Tree of Life within her would rejuvenate her by noontime and she would be back at full strength. The disease could harm her, but it could not kill her. It could cause pain, but it could not end her. There were days when she wished that it would end her. But the end never came.

Myrtle abandoned her quest to destroy other Trees of Life for the time being. Indeed, she began to think that it had been a mistake to destroy them at all. Would not a fresh fruit restore her fully? She opened her ears to old stories, but she was not so certain that she would put an axe to the next tree she found. That was assuming she had the strength for the journey. She was not so sure.

The years went by. She did everything she could to hide her predicament from her servants and friends. She spent everything she had to hire doctors or obtain medicines to cure her ailment. The last doctor had traded his best medicine for the title to her last estate. She only did this because the medicine had actually worked... for a year. But now she had nothing. It was not the first time that Myrtle had experienced despair in her long life, but it was certainly one of her lowest moments. Not knowing what else to do, she decided to make her way back to her home town. She entertained the silly idea that her husband might find her, having found another Tree of Life, and might share its healing goodness with her. She knew that, in fact, her husband would kill her, but deep down she knew that that was exactly what she wanted.

Travel was treacherous, but the Romans controlled the regions she was passing through these days, and they at least had good roads. They took her to Tarsus, and what she overheard there made her change her mind, and then her destination.

"I tell you, the man is the Messiah," one man was saying to

another.

"He does not do the things that the Messiah is expected to do," replied the other.

"He heals the sick and raises the dead. What more do you want?"

"A return of David's kingdom, which is precisely what the Scriptures say we should expect."

"Maybe that is coming. His ministry is young," replied the other.

"Young or not, he blasphemes by suggesting that he is something much more than the promised King. You yourself—who ought to know better—say he sounds like God Himself."

"I was there, Saul. When he fed the five thousand men, I was there. He took just a couple of loaves of bread, and blessed it, and with it, he fed all of us. You cannot believe how good that bread was! It smelled wonderful!"

Myrtle's attention had already been transfixed, but at this she nearly fell out of her seat in the marketplace. It now occurred to her that she was in the Jewish quarter. The food was kosher. The men had strange beards and garments. *And it was a Jew that had informed her and her husband about the Tree of Life.* Who was this man that they were now talking about?

"You say that there was only a handful of loaves. Obviously, there had to be more," Saul retorted.

The other man scoffed at him, "You are calling me a liar. After all my years of being truthful with you, you doubt me today. Aren't you the man of faith? Was it not Elijah who enjoyed the widow's bread day in and day out, even though there had only been a little? Do you believe this story, or not?"

"That's different."

"Different how?"

"Elijah didn't claim to be God."

"Because Elijah knew better. When you are able to make a little oil last on and on, you can tell us by what authority you do this. This man says he does it on his own authority. When you can do the same, you can tell us he is wrong."

"A false prophet, then."

"Who does signs such as these? He heals the sick, he raises

81

the dead..."

"Even if *he* rises from the dead, I will not believe! He's a blasphemer!"

"Or, he is who he says he is. What would persuade you?"

"I can think of nothing."

"Saul, Saul..."

Myrtle left them. She knew that the man being spoken of must be in Palestine, for that was where the Jewish country, Israel, was located. The man could heal the sick... and there was this tantalizing thing about bread. Might it be that he served bread to his people that was made from the fruit of the Tree of Life? She would not waste another minute wondering. She would go and find out for herself.

The closer she got to Jerusalem, the more people were talking about the man Jesus, especially, but not exclusively, in the Jewish areas. When she entered Judea proper, it was at a fever pitch. She overheard many arguments such as the one she heard in Tarsus. The one thing that was different was just how many people claimed to be eye witnesses of Jesus' miracles. Jesus had fed tens of thousands of people from just a few bits of bread and fish on several occasions. Jews had been raised from the dead, but so too had non-Jews. He had driven out demons. Some said that he had walked on water, but this had only been seen by his close associates. He was regarded by the leaders in the area as an enemy, but the people loved him... or the idea of him; on the latter there was confusion. Was he the next king of Israel, come to drive the Romans out and return Israel to a nation of prominence, ruled by God himself? Or was his agenda something else entirely?

Myrtle was quite prepared to stay out of that conversation. She was more interested in the man and what he could do for her, if he would do anything at all. What he meant to the Jews was none of her concern. She had learned by now that it was unwise to dismiss wild stories without investigation, but this was one of the few stories about 'miracle-men' that had seemed credible, and in the last twelve years, she'd heard quite a few of those stories, and investigated a goodly number of them, too. Jesus was *something*, if he was anything.

But as she joined the hordes that flocked to wherever Jesus was rumored to be, she realized that she could not ignore the question. The old stories of the Jews had proven to be true and changed the course of her life dramatically. She realized that if some of the new stories were true, there was no way she could continue to live as she had been living. She would have to re-orient her life. How? She was not so sure about that part.

When she finally was in the same town as he was, she had set aside the issue of what the Jews thought, and had reconciled herself *to believing Jesus*. Whatever Jesus said about himself, she was prepared to believe, because everywhere she went she heard more amazing stories, and it seemed every other person could say that they had had a first-hand encounter with Jesus. Was Jesus God? Was he merely a Jewish King? Myrtle was prepared to believe whichever Jesus himself said, because she now had every confidence that *the stories were true*.

Arriving in the same town as Jesus was one thing. Getting close enough to speak with him was a different story. She knew precisely where he was... within a thousand foot radius. The crowds pressed in all around him, and everyone had the same goal that she had: get to the Center. She observed this curious thing: people who had been perfectly healthy now suffered harm—elbowed, or trampled, or otherwise injured in the mob's mutual effort to get closer and closer. She felt pity for those who were not there out of mere curiosity, but had an actual ailment, as she did. It was hard for the weak to pry their way in.

She was close to despairing of the attempt (for today, anyway) when it became evident that the center of gravity of the mob had shifted in her direction. Jesus was coming her way!

She abandoned any hope of actually speaking with him, though. She would be fortunate enough to draw close enough to touch him.

"His touch..." she thought aloud. A man this powerful need not talk to her, or even be aware of her presence. If only she could just touch him, or the clothes he wore...

The mob steadily moved in her direction, and she realized that her moment had come. Throwing a few elbows of her own, she at last saw Jesus. She knew it was him, because everyone around him had his hands on her. His closest followers were vainly trying to give him space. She decided to capitalize on that, but even then it was nearly too late. He was past her!

She practically dove to the ground, slicing through the crowd like a rock through water, only this water offered much more resistance. She scraped her knees on the ground and someone's elbow caught her in the cheek on the way down, and another person's foot stepped on her arm, but with her other arm, she reached out... and touched the hem of his clothes.

It was as though she had once again partaken of the fruit of the Tree of Life. Immediately, her body grew warm. The ache on her cheek disappeared and the bruise on her arm (that she didn't even yet know about) faded away, and she knew in that instant that she had been healed, completely and utterly. The fruit of the Tree of Life had given her healing and strength, but in the course of her travels she had still met something that was able to deal a death blow to her; this man was stronger even than that. "He's the Man of Life," she intoned solemnly to herself.

But there was a problem.

"Who touched the master?"

People were looking around.

"Who touched me?" Jesus asked.

"The master says someone touched him—Master, really, look at all the people... see how many are touching you?"

"Who touched me?" Jesus asked again.

Myrtle fell to her knees, trembling. What had she done? She had taken advantage of a great man, quite against his will, consent, or even knowledge. She was nothing compared to this man, who was Everything. She had not received life from Jesus, she had stolen some from him. She deserved to be struck down. In fact, she welcomed it.

"These people press on me from all sides, but only you have touched me, woman. Tell me why you have touched me," Jesus said.

She knew that she had to tell the truth, for her sake, not for his. One look in his eyes, and she knew that he knew everything, anyway.

"I have been bleeding for twelve years, my Lord," she said.

"I've spent all that I have on doctors and medicine and had no more hope. I heard that there was a man in Israel who had Life, so I came. I touched you, and I was healed immediately."

"Daughter, your faith has healed you. Go in peace."

Just then, someone else broke in, speaking to a man near Jesus, "Your daughter is dead. Don't bother the teacher anymore."

Jesus frowned at the man speaking, but said to the one near him, "Don't be afraid; just believe, and she will be healed."

Myrtle's eyes met the man's eyes and found in them mutual understanding. She nodded to him as if to say, "She will indeed be healed, just as I was." The man nodded back to her, and turned to follow Jesus, who had already started walking away.

Myrtle allowed the mob to pass her by. Now completely healed and whole once again, she pondered her next step...

"You met Jesus?" Casey interjected, in shock.

"Face to face," Myrtle smiled.

"Were you there..."

"Yes, I stayed for quite awhile. I had one more conversation with him that perhaps I'll tell you about some day. It's enough for you to know that I was there right up to the end, *and after.* I even saw my husband there..." her voice grew soft. "But, obviously, we know how that story ended up. But for my part of it, I heeded the signs and fled the area while it was still possible to do so. I didn't go to my home village, but instead went north into what you know as Britain. That is because I learned of many tales about trees of power there. From there, you should know that I eventually ventured to the New World. Yes, I was here before the Vikings! I've been all over. The only one I did not destroy is the one that you have seen with your own eyes. You are not the first to have laid hold of a Gate Warden, you see. I caught one myself a thousand years ago! I learned a great deal at that time, as you can well understand, and their special protections have been applied to the tree you have seen. It is safe and will remain safe so long as the Wardens exist to defend it. Unfortunately, I know that at least one tree has escaped my detection, for I know that my husband lives to this day, wreaking havoc wherever he applies his thought. This tree, or *these* trees if there are more than one, must be found and it must be destroyed. That is part of your task, young Casey."

"Wow," I repeated.

Myrtle was not done, though. "I should add," she continued, "that I have not yet been able to find the Tree of Knowledge of Good and Evil, either. It is my belief that part of my husband's enduring power and influence comes from him feasting on it. We must find it, too, and destroy it."

"And?" Mr. Chaffee prompted.

Myrtle fixed her eyes sternly on mine and declared, "And we must 'un-con-sti-tute' my husband if we get the chance, while we are at it!"

"You may not have noticed," I said slowly, "but I am only twelve-years old."

"You are no average twelve-year old," she said firmly. There was a hint of anger in her voice, as if she were tired of me saying such things. "First of all, you are of my line. There is a trace of my vigor in your blood. Second of all, you have spent time with the Wardens. Your eyes will be open to things others can't see. You will not regard everything you hear as impossibilities without further investigation. You know enough now to take everything seriously, pending the evidence. Third of all, precisely because you are twelve-years old, you will likely escape the notice of my husband during his hunts."

"During... his... hunts?" I stammered.

"That's right, young Casey. He has been hunting me for thousands of years. We are arch enemies. He knows that I stand opposed to his goals and that I, and perhaps I alone, can resist or even overthrow him. He knows, too, that the Wardens exist—no doubt a result of his eating of the Tree of Knowledge of Good and Evil—and he at least suspects that they are concealing me, if he doesn't also suspect they are hiding the Tree of Life as well. He hunts Wardens, too. He has killed many, but we do not believe he has found where they live. The moment that he knows that you exist, Casey, he will hunt you, as well. If you throw your lot in with us, you risk violent death. Do you understand what I am asking of you?" Myrtle put to me.

"I do," I said, more bravely than I felt. "How do we start?

86

How will we find him? You haven't even told me his name!"

"Oh, you know at least one of his names, young Casey," Myrtle stated mysteriously, a small, knowing smile on her face.

"I do?"

"Indeed. You will know him from the history books as Vlad the Impaler."

I tried hard to remember anything about such a person but couldn't think of anything. I confessed, "I'm sorry, Myrtle, but I don't know that name."

"Oh, yes you do," she retorted. "Vlad the Impaler's other, more famous name, is Count Dracula. When he was my husband, his name was Draco."

"Your husband... is a vampire?" I said, trembling slightly.

"He is the source of many of the vampire legends, but he is not a vampire as understood in the popular sense," Myrtle explained.

"He is virtually immortal," Mr. Chaffee pointed out.

"Yes, that's true," Myrtle acceded.

"And, he has a very unhealthy interest in blood," Mr. Chaffee reminded her.

"Well, yes. But he doesn't bite people's neck and suck their blood, turn into a bat, and that sort of thing. A stake through the heart wouldn't do anything to him, either, except cause him a great deal of pain and make him extremely angry, which, when he was healed, he would act upon," Myrtle rebutted.

"Unhealthy interest... in blood?" I stammered.

Myrtle's demeanor was grim.

"This no doubt stems from the fact that he has eaten of the Tree of Knowledge of Good and Evil. He has what we would call a 'morbid curiosity' in general. In other words, he has an *unhealthy* interest in *everything*. In some respects, the image of the so-called 'mad scientist' suits him well. We might imagine that it is possible to kill something just for the sake of dissecting it and consider it a morally sane thing to do. But to take pleasure in the killing itself? That's an illness. My husband, I'm afraid, takes pleasure in *not* killing, if you catch my meaning," Myrtle related.

"But, blood?" I pressed. I was still fixated on the notion that Myrtle's husband was an honest-to-goodness vampire.

Myrtle sighed.

"I said that I was there to meet Jesus and remained in the area where he died and rose again. I said also that I met my husband there. Indeed, he was in the crowd when I was healed, and he heard my story. I believe that was the first time it occurred to him that blood might be significant; in particular, *my* blood. But he must have concluded that as powerful as my blood might be, the blood of the healer must be 'off the charts,' as they say. Remember, he and I were both there to be instructed by the Jewish teacher centuries earlier, 'The life of a creature is in its blood.' He no doubt reasoned that the blood of Christ would fix all; one had to eat of the Tree of Life over and over, even if it was separated by hundreds of years, but there is Blood that'll do the job once and for all and grant life everlasting, *even if one dies*," Myrtle explained.

"So, he hopes to lay his hands on the blood of Jesus?" I asked, confused.

"That's right," she replied. "Now, my first inclination is that if he succeeded, it would spell his immediate doom. What fellowship does light have with the darkness? Surely there must be some 'deep magic' that would prevent Christ's blood from having the effect my husband desires. On the other hand, it is just because the power in Christ's blood is an objective reality that is not subject to the whims of Man that I am afraid the effect will be more terrible for us than him, at least in the short term."

"You don't think God would give Draco eternal life even though he would still be an evil man, do you?" I worried.

"Oh, I should say definitely not!" Myrtle laughed. "And, yet, Jesus said that his kingdom was like a field where an enemy had come and planted weeds among the good seed. Instead of pulling up the whole field, he told his workers to let the harvest come, and then sort things out. In other words, I believe that God would let human decision unfold right up to the very end, despite the horrific consequences that may follow. There will come a day when he will set things right. In the meantime, we must do our best to do good in the world, and resist evil where we may. There are some horrific consequences that we may be able to prevent."

I felt creeping into my heart a spreading fear. My good sense told me that I really ought to think carefully about signing on for these tasks, but with precious Myrtle sitting just a few feet away from me, brimming with life, I knew that I would never again find a cause so unambiguously noble, pure, and proper. Still, this was much more than I had bargained for. I confess that I was frightened.

"You mean for me to help you keep Draco from getting Jesus' blood?" I whispered.

"That's right," Myrtle nodded. She seemed sad as she said it, as though even if they succeeded it could very well come at a great cost. Or, perhaps, that it *would* come at a great cost.

# Chapter 17

I assured Myrtle that I was committed to the project, but it didn't take very long for me to begin having doubts. I don't know what I expected, exactly, but I guess I assumed our quest would begin in a museum, perhaps, or maybe a crypt. Instead, my dear friend Marmor fetched me and took me once again into the crystal tunnels where we journeyed for what seemed a very, very long time. When finally he split the seam in the sky and bid me step out into the world I was most familiar with, I knew immediately that we had not simply traversed the planet. My gut told me that we had once again gone back in time. When Marmor told me that this time we had bridged two thousand years, I knew he told me the truth. Even so, I grew dizzy, and had to sit down on a large boulder—one of many strewn about the wilderness we now found ourselves in.

"Marmor... where are we? *When* are we?" I asked plaintively.

"Have you not guessed?" he replied.

"Tell me anyway," I said.

"We are in a place that in your own day is called Israel or Palestine, and the time is early in the first century. Indeed, to be more precise, about twenty-four hours from now, a certain Jesus, called the Christ, will be crucified. You are not more than two or three hours away from where this will happen," Marmor explained, watching my expression closely.

I put my face in my hands and put my head between my knees. I was overwhelmed by the thought that I might actually witness what millions of people had only read about. Marmor put his big hands on my back, and with the warmth of his touch also came the special touch of the Wardens. I lifted my head.

"What are we to do? We cannot change time, right? Isn't that what I learned when I saw myself in my own house and yard?" I asked.

"I have told you that these are the deep things, not easily understood even by my race, let alone the human race. The important thing to remember is that 'past,' 'present,' and 'future' are words that humans use to describe reality as they perceive it, but in point of fact, there is in reality no such thing as 'past' or 'future.' There is only 'present.' What you call your 'past' is only your present recollection of past 'presents.' The Wardens are able to step in and out of other 'presents,' while humans are not; you are a special case. But God sees all 'presents' simultaneously. In this light, in principle at least, it is not anymore astounding that one could impact a 'past' present than one is able to affect a 'present' present," Marmor said.

"But that doesn't answer my question," I said.

"Just as once you were given sight so that you could see our great caverns, so also you have been now given the full measure of reality as the *Wardens* perceive it," Marmor said. "It is a temporary dispensation, while you are with me and in Myrtle's service."

"How does it work?" I asked.

"The low cannot go up except by being within something higher as it makes its ascent, but the high may go to the low."

Sometimes Marmor infuriated me.

"You're not helping," I stamped my feet.

"Through technology, you might perhaps be able to see the world as a fly sees it, but there is no hope for the fly that it will be able to create technology that will allow it to see the world as the sons of Adam perceive it. Through your imagination and the creation of mental models, you are able to explore the fabric of reality itself, what you refer to as atoms. But atoms themselves can imagine nothing."

I began to really stew now, and Marmor could tell I was at the limits of my patience.

"Very well, then," he said. "Think of it this way. It is a matter of perspective. Time is very much like a book. For the characters of the book, the narrative is linear, and time appears to proceed word by word, sentence by sentence, and page by page; in English, that is from left to right, top to bottom, and left to right again. Without your special dispensation, you experience time just like that, as one of the characters locked into the two dimensional page. With your special dispensation, however, you are more like the reader, who can open the book to any page he pleases at any time, and read the story at that moment, experiencing past and future 'presents' always as 'present' from your own perspective."

"But a book cannot be changed," I protested.

"No? Authors do it all the time," Marmor said.

"Am I an author?" I asked.

"In a manner, yes. Every human is. That's the beauty of what the theologians call 'free-will.' But you are being permitted to experience another level of will, wherein you and I can leave the 'page' that is your own time, and 'flip back' to a previous page, and insert ourselves back into the page as characters on it, scribbling our revisions on it, and, consequently, altering various aspects of the Story itself."

"But, what if we break something, and in the future..."

"A future 'present'..." Marmor corrected me.

"...In a 'future' present, I prevent my own birth!" I said.

"You are an author, sure, but you are not *the* Author. You are made in *the image* of the Author. If we can flip back and forth in the book so as to see this page and now that page, the Author sees all pages, all moments, simultaneously. It is rightly said that the Author knows all, because in point of fact, He *sees* all. 'Revisions' are known before they happen, because for Him, there is no 'before.' You are sustained by *His* powerful word... not your own."

I did not find Marmor's explanations very comforting, let alone comprehensible, but it was evident that whether I understood how it all worked or not, I was nonetheless in the dusty wilderness a short walk from Jerusalem, not long before Christ was to be crucified. There remained the question of what I was actually supposed to do. I didn't have a chance to ask. Marmor looked to the sky with an expectant look.

"Behold, dear Casey; you are about to see that which is not for the children of Adam to see until long after the final reckoning. Even I, who have known of this moment as one of the great moments in the history of the Gate Wardens, have not yet actually been *in* the moment. Be silent, and watch."

***

Whatever I was supposed to see did not happen immediately. I allowed my eyes to wander, inspecting the barren landscape and watching whirling, spiraling dust clouds spring up spontaneously only to disappear just as quickly. If one can believe it, for the first time I noticed that I was wearing the garb common for the period. I observed that I was wearing rudimentary sandals and fell to considering how it was possible that my feet could so quickly become caked with so much dust.

After a time, I began to perceive that the wind was picking up, and the twisting dust clouds did not dissipate so quickly as before. Soon, twigs and bramble began floating across the ground, chased by small rocks that tumbled along behind them. Finally, the wind was gusting hard enough that I realized I might very well be in danger. Grains of sand flew into my face, stinging my cheeks and finding their way into my nostrils and mouth. With the building wind speed came a growing rumble, and then a roar. Quite unintentionally, I clung to Marmor's thick arm. The hair, I was reminded, was as soft as a lamb's ear. It did not seem compatible with a creature such as Marmor, who would scare the uninitiated to death with a glance. Marmor was smiling as if he was bathing in pleasure itself.

Just when it seemed that I could not bear it any further, a bright white line of light appeared in the sky, looking for all the world like a second horizon atop the horizon I was accustomed to, only closer. The line grew brighter, and wider, until not even the light of the sun could compete. I had seen the doors of heaven before. This was something like that, only not a door, but a highway; more than that, a great expanse. As the expanse opened, great gusts of air blew out from it, scraping the landscape so bare of things that could be tossed that within just a few short moments the only hint of the wind was the noise it was making. One can only see the wind when there are things being carried along in it, and there was nothing left to be carried away.

It was at that moment that creatures began stepping out of the chasm of light. They were other Wardens. All the ones I had seen before had been decked out majestically, to be sure, but these were clearly marked for war. The Wardens had no use for weapons in the sense that we use objects to inflict or deflect violence, but even so it seemed that they had breastplates that shone brightly from their chests and shields of light fixed to their arms. From their heads flowed long strands of hair like the Wardens I was familiar with, but the color of the hair was a blazing white. The contrast with the dark brown color of the rest of their body was striking. I had always had trouble distinguishing the Warden 'fur' from clothing; I perceived that in this instance what I took to be white hair was in fact some kind of helmet.

They stepped out of the light in unison, right foot followed by the left, and then they marched forward in a line until they were a short distance from the sky-schism. Each step resounded like one boulder falling upon another. They stood in formation like this all the while angels of God thundered out of the opening like so much liquid light.

I would have expected the angels to be as orderly as the keepers of the gates, and perhaps on other occasions they were, but in this instance they fell out of the space in great rivulets, running wild in all directions. Some of them seemed to be riding upon beasts, or trailing behind in what I can best describe as chariots. The last to emerge from out of the expanse were several dozen giant angels astride, as my mind could best make out, on flashes of lightning crudely shaped like dragons.

Then, there was a great sucking sound, and the gate was closed in a rush. The Warden-warriors threw their backs against the sky as a unit. There was the muffled sound of some other entities trying to break into the world as I knew it, like someone knocking violently against a door, but far away, and to no effect. After some time, the violence ceased. The Warden-warriors disappeared in a flash. The only signs that anything had just happened at that spot were a landscape that had been blown clean of all debris, a heavenly smell, and young, ancient, beautiful Myrtle, sitting on a stone, smiling at me.

# Chapter 18

"We stand on the fulcrum upon which all of human history rests. Why be surprised that all of the armies of the universe are present in force at it?" Myrtle said, anticipating my question.

"I suppose I never thought about it," said I.

"A problem endemic to all of us," she replied. "Come now, there isn't much time!"

***

Myrtle picked a point on the horizon and told me that Jerusalem lay just on the other side of it and bid me follow her across the wild plain. It was hard to keep up. Like me, she was clothed in the garb of the day. I longed for a good pair of tennis shoes or hiking boots and wondered if she did as well, but then remembered that she lived for hundreds of years before such comforts had been invented.

"What about Marmor?" I said, once I realized he was no longer with us.

"He has his own appointed duties," she replied, with a tone that implied I should have known the answer before I even asked. I said nothing, and continued the difficult work of merely keeping pace with her.

"What are we going to do when we get to Jerusalem?" I asked.

Myrtle breathed out a sigh of exhaustion which wasn't from the walking.

"How are we going to stop your husband? How will we even find him?"

"Everything you need to know will be made known *when* you need it. Can we just get there, first?" she said curtly. Her tone of voice reminded me of the one my parents had sometimes taken.

I shrugged, and fell silent.

After about an hour, we found a road. It was nothing like the roads I was accustomed to and only believed it was a road because Myrtle insisted that it was. Before too long, we saw others on the road, as well. The closer we got to Jerusalem, the more people we saw. Not only the road was more crowded, but also the areas immediate to the road and a little further off. There were many who had stopped to rest alongside the road, but many more that had set up camps a stone's throw from it.

Not long after this, I found that we were walking in a veritable throng.

"Is it always this crowded?" I whispered to Myrtle.

"It is when it is the Passover. A population of a small American city swells to the size of a great one, like Chicago or New York. Jerusalem is the only place the Jews can lawfully offer sacrifices, so they must come if that is their desire. Now be quiet; you'll attract attention."

Through some mysterious work, I had been clothed with the same things that first century Jews wore, but we were still speaking English. It was not as much of a concern as one would think at first blush. I could hear all around me people speaking in many diverse languages. I discerned that many must have come from very far away. I thought about how weary I had become after just a couple of hours of travel and realized the Passover must be a very big deal.

After what seemed to be an eternity of small, barely perceptible movements, we arrived at our destination. Myrtle led me through one of Jerusalem's gates, down some of its twisting alleys, and, still pushing and shoving through the masses, into what was probably the only isolated corner left. It was a small residence tucked away at the rear of a larger residence which Myrtle said she had rented. It had the advantage of having its own private entrance and was sealed off from the rest of the structure, allowing us a measure of privacy.

"You rented this?"

"The Myrtle of two thousand years ago did," she replied.

"And what if she returns?" I laughed.

"She won't. I know where she is right now," Myrtle smiled.

"How can you remember it with that kind of precision? I don't even know where I was three days ago!" I said.

"Tonight is the night that Yeshua will be betrayed. That sort of thing is easy to remember," she said. Myrtle allowed me to ponder the significance of the situation for a few moments but finally broke into my contemplation, "Now, we must talk about what must be done."

"I am listening."

"We must find my husband and prevent him from laying hold of even a single drop of Jesus' blood," she began. "He will recognize me, which will be a hindrance to our cause. He would not recognize you, however. Also, I am a woman, and in this time and place there are certain boundaries I am compelled to respect. You will be able to get into places he might be found that I cannot."

"Such as?"

"Think."

So, I did.

"Alright," I said, straining to recollect details from Jesus' trial and crucifixion. "After Jesus was arrested, he was struck during his first trial before the Jewish leaders. There may be blood there. Then he would have been beaten by the Roman guards at the hands of Pontius Pilate. I suppose at any point in the path that Jesus took while carrying his cross there may have been blood. At the crucifixion itself, of course."

"Very good," Myrtle said. "Now, my husband is a crafty man, but he is not a supernatural being. He will not be able to access all these locations simultaneously. We have the advantage of knowing in advance where Jesus will be at certain times. We will get there first and watch for him. If we see him trying to obtain blood, we must try to stop him, at any cost."

"I'm ready," I said.

"There are two things I must mention," she said, adopting an even more serious tone than the one she had already been employing. I nodded to indicate I was listening, and she continued. "There is a very good chance that we may have to split up, and you may become lost. No one will understand you if you ask for help—no one, that is, who could possibly be on our side. You do not know Greek, the language that all those under Roman rule must speak, or Aramaic, the language that the people here speak, in addition to Greek. But do not fear. There are some things that are appointed for us, and one of them is our departure. No matter where we are at or what we are doing, at just the right time, the Wardens will fetch us and return us to the time you properly belong."

"Hopefully I won't starve to death while waiting," I joked. But Myrtle wasn't laughing.

"The other thing you must know is this: It is not only the heavenly host that is assembled for this event. There is the reality you can see, but a deeper one that you can't. The battle is joined across both of them. You must never forget that there is an Enemy greater than my husband. To this Enemy, my husband is of very small concern at present, because this Enemy 'has other fish to fry,' as it were. Neither my husband nor the Enemy knows how this is going to end. Indeed, the Enemy is presently engaged in bending minds and wills to the cause of Jesus' arrest and murder, thinking that this will complete his victory over the World, not knowing that in fact it will accomplish the exact opposite."

I felt a shiver run through my body as what Myrtle was saying settled in.

She continued, "It is imperative that we do nothing to alter this great fact. I doubt very much that our meddling would be allowed to change the grand scheme of things, but we may do great harm as far as the details go. You do not want the Enemy's eye to fall upon you! Nor can we allow my husband to guess at the outcome, or, if it were possible, something worse: surmise that some kind of traveling to past or future 'presents' were possible to mortals!"

Now I trembled. Not very long ago, I was just a child wandering around my yard. Today, I was in a place where I might somehow affect the salvation of countless souls—for the worse. It did not seem proper, or wise, to have involved me. I fought back a feeling of resentment to have put me in this situation, remembering that I had essentially volunteered for it. But I had not known the stakes!

Myrtle continued, "It is for this reason that you can only communicate in your native language. It would have been as easy to let you speak Greek or Aramaic as it was for Mammal to give you Sight, but in this way, we do not have to worry that you may say something that Draco could overhear, to our peril. Also,

American English is thousands of years off. While I'm sure my husband would find your dialect very curious, it is extremely unlikely that he would guess it comes from a 'present' that is so far distant from him. As for the Enemy..."

"Yes?"

"Well, he can't read minds, and his own will be focused on Someone else. I don't know precisely what he could gather from attending to you, but even so, let's try to be discrete," she said.

I was far from comforted. In the back of my mind, however, I sensed that between the two of us, Myrtle was less concerned about *me* falling into enemy hands than she was about *her* falling into enemy hands. It would be an intelligence windfall.

"Now, get some rest. In just a couple of hours, Yeshua will be betrayed, and we need to be in position."

I laid down on the bed of straw and closed my eyes. I didn't think I could possibly sleep, but I did.

# Chapter 19

I was shaken awake. My eyes opened and met the twinkling, near-angelic, eyes of Myrtle.

"It is time," she said.

She busied herself with last minute preparations as I slowly became alert. Soon, we were out the door, making our way through the crowded streets of Jerusalem.

"As we speak," she said, "Yeshua is with his disciples, celebrating the Passover meal and making his own changes to it. After that, the Garden of Gethsemane. I don't know exactly where they are having the meal, but I do know where the garden is. We'll intercept them there."

Since I had been instructed to remain silent, I merely nodded.

Dusk was nearly upon us when we finally stopped to rest, just outside the city, halfway up what Myrtle told me was the Mount of Olives. All around us, indeed, all around Jerusalem itself, were rudimentary shelters and tents. It was quiet, though, as families performed the Passover rites to the best of their ability given their circumstances. There were still plenty of people about, but the numbers had certainly diminished. For all intents and purposes, therefore, we were once again alone.

"Myrtle, how will I know how to recognize your husband? I don't even know what he looks like," I reminded her. The problem was compounded by the fact that all of the men of the town were similarly adorned, required by ceremonial law to be dressed and groomed in a particular way. It occurred to me then that between the common way that all the men were dressed and the great mass of people that was strewn about, even unto the hills, it was no wonder that Jesus' enemies needed a betrayer to identify the place where Jesus would be, and also exactly who he was, especially now that it was beginning to get dark.

"He will not be easy to spot, even for me," Myrtle said. "Watch for someone paying unusual attention to Jesus' blood or wounds. That is the best we can do."

"I know that we have the advantage of knowing where Jesus will be, but you know, he was kinda all over the place. We won't be able to watch every spot," I said.

"But, we will have made our best effort, and that is all that can be asked," Myrtle said. "Very little—if anything—that occurs is not somehow appointed. All the more in this present hour."

I nodded.

***

"There!" Myrtle blurted out, doing her best to keep her voice down. "That is almost certainly Yeshua and his disciples."

I could see the forms of about a dozen men winding their way towards us. We were seated in such a way that they could pass by without catching their attention, or even the attention of someone who may have been trailing them. For this reason, when they came past us, I could not make out which one was Jesus, or really distinguish any of them, one from another. Nor did I see anyone following them.

Once they had passed and disappeared from sight, Myrtle whispered to me, "They will be coming back down. According to the Scriptures, when Jesus prayed he was in such torment that his sweat was like great drops of blood. No doubt, this was just a turn of phrase. Just in case, though, I'm going to try to get closer. You stay here and watch for anyone trying to sneak up the mountain. If I do not return in time to see Yeshua being led to his first trial, you should try to follow."

Despite the full moon beginning to make its existence known, the thought of being alone in a strange city terrified me. The fact that it was dark did not help. Myrtle smiled at me with that beatific way she had, and I felt courage surge through me. She put her hand on my shoulder, and disappeared into the olive grove.

***

A couple of hours after Jesus and the disciples went into the garden, I spied a large band of armed men with blazing torches making its way out of the city and up towards the garden. This was, no doubt, the party tasked with arresting Jesus. The train of light would be impossible to miss to those further up the hill.

Anyone who guessed the party's intent would easily have time to escape, but I knew that the object of their intent had no intention of evading them.

I could see the torchlight dancing between the branches of the grove, albeit from a great distance. I knew that the first wave of disciples would have already deserted Jesus, but I was surprised that they didn't come by me. I then remembered that the mountain had another side to it, and that prior to coming to Jerusalem, Jesus and his disciples had stayed in Bethany. Perhaps that city was on the other side of the mountain, and the disciples fled that way rather than risk their own arrest in Jerusalem.

The torchlight began winding its way towards me. My chest tightened in apprehension. As it passed nearest to me, I hunkered down between some boulders, behind a tree. Despite the moon light and the torchlight, it was impossible to make out which one was Jesus. I let them all go by me and then waited a little longer for Myrtle. When it seemed that she would not be coming, I became filled with panic, firstly, because I had indeed been left alone, and secondly, because I knew if I didn't act now, I would lose the party in the city.

I gathered up my courage and leapt from my place and jogged towards the path. Just as I stepped on it, I was knocked to the ground. I had startled a man who was likewise trailing at a distance. At this distance, and in this light, he was much easier to make out than the others. I couldn't help but think he was... glowing? As he sprinted off, muttering in some language I did not comprehend, I realized with a start what I was likely seeing. "If I didn't know better, that man was wearing no clothes..." I murmured.

I let the madman get well ahead of me and then continued my pursuit of the arresting party. But it was too late. There were many people about with torches, and I had no idea which way the ones I was interested in had gone. Nor did I know their final destination, in order to catch them there. Without that information, and the company of Myrtle, I was like a ship without a rudder.

Remembering Myrtle's words about at least making an effort, I wandered aimlessly around the narrow streets of Jerusalem.

People were everywhere going about their business. The temperature was crisp but bearable, the wind was still, the sky was clear. Even so, my breathing tightened as if the atmosphere itself was pressing in on me. The space around me seemed to constrict as I contemplated the events that were unfolding at that very hour—momentous, life-altering events—and my own failure to accomplished the task that had been set before me.

"If nothing else, to be able to actually see these things for myself..." I whispered. Alas, I could not find where Jesus was presently being tried. I needed a good, old fashioned map. "Or," I thought to myself, "a good, old fashioned education on Jerusalem in the first century." Since both were lacking, I hoped Myrtle would find me soon. Preferably, before her husband found me.

# Chapter 20

Alone and lost in Jerusalem, I was forced to find the best shelter I could, given the circumstances. I don't know what was worse: abject failure in regards to my quest, or the steady drop in the temperature which made it far too chilly to sleep comfortably. All night long, I waited for the sun, looking forward to it in a way I could not recall ever doing so before. When the sun did in fact break over the horizon, bringing me some much needed warmth, I remembered that it was 'Good Friday.' However Jesus had spent the night, I had a feeling that he had a much different reaction to the dawn.

The noise level in the town began to increase as people woke up and stoked their fires. After a time, however, there was a different kind of noise. It didn't take me long to figure out that the residents and visitors of Jerusalem had learned of Jesus' arrest. I observed numerous excited conversations, and their frequency and intensity increased as the morning warmed up. Some people seemed to be merely curious. Others were mournful. Many others seemed nervous. I discerned that a goodly number were forgoing their previous plans for the morning and were heading to the scene of Jesus' trial before Pontius Pilate, so I discretely followed some until I had a good sense of where the thing was going down.

Though I knew what I might see would be gruesome, I also knew it was profoundly historic. More than that—if I believed what I said I believed—it would be an opportunity to put my own eyes on God Himself, incarnate in the world. Would he lock eyes with me, if only I was properly positioned?

I longed to know, but it became clear it was not going to happen. Inside the place where Jesus was being tried, there were innumerable men yelling and shouting out against Jesus, and presumably, Pilate. Outside, though, there were people visibly upset by the proceedings. As word was passed along in ripples through the crowd, I could tell that many of them were crushed by the news, their hope dashed right before my eyes. I wished to comfort them with what I knew; my tongue had been tied to prevent just that. At any rate, with all these people vying to get close to the action, there was no way I could get close enough to set eyes on Jesus. I could only hope that Myrtle's husband was having the same difficulty.

It hardly seemed possible for the crowds to get any bigger or the people more impassioned, but that is precisely what happened. Also, I had somehow gotten the impression from my upbringing that the trial had happened relatively quickly, but in fact it seemed to go on and on, and there was far more discourse than I had expected. At one point, Jesus was led away. The crowds dissipated. When Jesus returned from his time with King Herod, the crowds grew to a large size again. The Jewish leaders and their sympathizers were increasingly irate, as if they were surprised at the difficulty they were having. Even without following the conversation, or even hearing anything other than shouts, I had the sense that their anger was not only directed at Jesus, but also reflected a sense of betrayal, as though perhaps Pilate had originally agreed to do one thing for them but was now looking for a way to weasel out of the agreement. I decided that when, if, I made it back to my own 'present,' I would look again at the Scriptures to see if there was insight on this.

As the shouting intensified, even I was able to discern what they were saying: "Crucify him!" It soon became plain that matters had come to a head, and Jesus was about to be scourged, because I could hear women sobbing, and soon after that, the sounds of lashes and crude men laughing. I remembered that here, too, there would be blood. I put myself on the look-out, but as was the case earlier, it seemed impossible for any unauthorized person to draw near to Jesus. One was lucky—if that is the word—to even come close enough to see him.

I knew that after this, Jesus would be led to the place of the crucifixion, and this route had been immortalized in tradition. That didn't mean that I knew the route, however. Jesus' blood could conceivably fall anywhere on that route, and for all I knew, a mere drop would suffice for Draco's purposes. I felt once again thwarted by my ignorance. I did not know the language. I did not know the city. I did not know the culture. I did not know the context of the times. My father had tried to teach me such things, and I had wasted precious time resisting his efforts. I was

105

now paying the price.

"And if Draco gets any of that blood, who knows how many thousands or even millions will pay the price," I said ruefully.

I sensed the crowd shifting position. Jesus was certainly on his way to Golgotha now. My only play was to hope I got lucky. I had some faint recollection that the place of the crucifixion was outside the city walls, because Jewish custom forbade such things from happening within the Holy City. I reasoned that if I tracked the crowd while moving roughly towards the city's edge, I'd have a good chance of stumbling over the route. If I did, would Jesus look at me? What would it mean if he did?

I had to see him. I *had* to.

***

My strategy worked, in that I was able to discern Jesus' route. It could not put me directly on Jesus' path, though. There were just too many people. I could sometimes catch glimpses of the journey between the buildings, but that was the best I could do. I had been within five hundred feet of Jesus for many, many hours, and had not yet actually seen him!

It occurred to me after forty minutes of stalking the route that the job I had been assigned did not require anticipating where Jesus would be and then arriving their first. I now saw that I had been trying to do that with my own interests in mind. When I remembered my task, I realized that blood-trace would be left *behind* Jesus as he made his trip, and not, obviously, ahead of him. Moreover, Myrtle's husband would almost certainly be ignorant of the route, and would not even be able to appeal to two thousand years of tradition as a guide. He would be compelled to follow behind Jesus. If this was Draco's tact, he had a significant head start—unless, of course, he had already succeeded in his aim.

I doubled back and squeezed through some buildings until I came to the rocky alley that I was sure Jesus had journeyed on. There was still a steady stream of people trailing behind Jesus, although there were a few moving against the current, engaged in their normal course of business. I moved along with the current, keeping my eyes on the ground and trying to stay out of the way of those walking against me. After just a moment, I saw a dark splotch on the ground, and knew it must be blood.

Jesus' blood.

There, in the middle of that alley, with dozens and hundreds of people around and practically over me, was the blood of Jesus. I knelt down next to it, bending over so that I could look at it more closely.

A thought suddenly occurred to me.

"Draco thinks he can do something with this blood... according to what I've learned, this blood represents the salvation of mankind. Why shouldn't *I* collect some...?"

If Draco could harm countless people with this blood, what could I, someone with good intentions, do with it? I looked about for a way to collect the blood. It was a small pool that had soaked the top layer of the sand. It wasn't much, but if I found a suitable way to contain it, I could add to it from what I find further along. About ten feet away, I found a clay pot that looked like it could hold two or three gallons. When I was sure no one was looking, I snatched it and returned to the place where the blood was. I carefully scraped the top layer into the pot. Job complete, I continued along the path in search of more spots.

It was not as easy as one might suppose. Probably, there were numerous droplets strewn along the way, but with the crowds trampling over it for at least twenty minutes or so, these smaller deposits would be quickly obliterated. At any rate, I did not see very many drops of blood. I wondered if there was some metaphysical significance to the people of Jerusalem stomping all over Jesus' blood, like so many feet stomping out the juice from grapes.

No one noticed me as I stooped down in several places to scoop some more bloody dirt into the pot. It was about half full already when I found a very large spot. "Jesus must have fallen down here," I said to myself. I greedily scraped as much as I could into the pot and continued on.

I passed through a gate and was now outside the city walls. Sure enough, I could see that a crowd had gathered not far away. I could hear shouts of agony and angry shouts of contempt. I realized that if I could just find the place where they had pounded the nails through Jesus' feet and hands, I would find a veritable mother lode of the elixir of life I was gathering. I threaded my way around the edges of the crowd to where I guessed the Romans had done their work. I kept my eyes to the ground, lest I overlook another precious deposit.

"Here!" I exclaimed.

And then... "Father forgive them, for they know not what they do..."

I seemed to hear the words inside my skull, but they were loud and clear. I remembered suddenly where I was, and who was here. I was about to turn my eyes to the cross when I heard...

"Draco. Draco, stop. Give me the jar. Stop."

It was Myrtle, and she was talking to *me*.

***

"*I* am Draco..." I said aloud, the realization piercing me to the core. Then the universe faded away, and a heavy blanket fell upon my consciousness.

# Chapter 21

When I awoke, I felt as though I had been sleeping for ages. Not just any sleep, but a deep, satisfying sleep. I was completely rested. I blinked my eyes, trying to figure out where I was.

It was not Jerusalem.

It was not my home.

It was not the realm of the Wardens.

It was not the dingy house in New York.

There were two quaint, old fashioned windows in the room, and each was open, allowing a refreshing wind to come in and touch my cheek. An antique chair was in one corner, and next to it, an antique desk with a candlestick on it.

I patted my body to make sure I was all present and accounted for.

"Where am I?" I said.

"You know where you are," came the sweet voice.

I did; I was in Myrtle's home.

"Where are you?"

"Look."

My eyes roamed the room and then beheld that the chair had an occupant. Through some enchantment, I hadn't seen Myrtle sitting there before. Even now, it was only as she stood up and approached me that I was able to discern that it was her. It was though the chair had blossomed, and Myrtle the flower. Now I remembered: it was in Myrtle's room, and this was the bed of revival.

Another question now came to my mind.

"Am I... Draco?"

Myrtle hesitated, and then said, "*Are* you?"

"I... I didn't *think* so."

"There you have it, then," she replied. "Only, you forget that you are, though from across the generations, my grandson; likewise, you are also *his* grandson. There was a moment there, with the noon light just right, where I saw the family resemblance."

I let that sink in.

"But... and... well, the jar?" I stammered.

"I had to give it up in order to save you," Myrtle explained.

109

"Do you... will you... forgive me?" I pleaded.

"For what?" she asked me. "If anything, I should be asking for your forgiveness."

"I don't see how..."

"The Enemy was present in all his strength. His eye was not on you, but there were other eyes. There were many instruments. Some volunteered themselves, others were taken by force. I didn't prepare you well enough. There was no time. This almost proved your undoing. Will you forgive *me*?" she asked.

If you could have seen her pleading eyes, you would know why I could not refuse. I nodded my assent, weakly, as though overcome by a powerful request.

"I... at first, all I wanted to do was see Jesus face to face. Then, all my thoughts were on the 'good' I could do with Jesus' blood. But it didn't seem right, and I couldn't put my finger on why." I started to weep; billions of people have lived and died, wishing above all else that they could see Jesus face to face, and there I was, a scant dozen yards or so away on several occasions and never once succeeded. In the end, it was by my own volition.

Myrtle put her arm around my shoulders. After I had calmed down some, she began speaking in soothing tones, reminding me of the supernatural cleverness of the Enemy and also the supernatural forgiveness of the Father.

I stood up and walked to the window and looked out at the lovely estate that was sprawled out before me. I recalled the first time that I had laid eyes on this scene. There had been angels of dark and light locked into mortal combat here, there, everywhere. Occasionally, a Warden was caught in the crossfire, and was stricken. What was unseen had been more monumental than what was seen. Surely it was the same even now, where I stood? Surely, two thousand years ago, if I had had eyes to see it, I could have seen the clash of ages? Through mysterious workings, I had been there too, and I was one of many, assuredly, that had been caught in the crossfire.

I would understand it all at the end of all things.

Even so, I knew that it would take me some time to be healed. Even now, the humiliation of being taken in burned at me. I was still ashamed that the jar containing Jesus' blood had been lost on my account. And then there was the realization that Draco's blood ran through me just as certainly as Myrtle's blood did. This fact had been true all along and yet I had never considered it. I now felt that I must give the fact some weight.

In the meantime, Myrtle offered her eyes to me as a comfort, and these thoughts drifted off to the back of my mind. Hot chocolate had been produced somehow, which I sipped carefully. After a time, Myrtle excused herself and bid me to come to the dining room when I was ready. I finished off the hot chocolate and made my way down the familiar staircase, reaching out with my hand to touch, if I could, an unseen tree that I knew nonetheless was really there.

Myrtle was waiting for me at the table, joined by Mr. Chaffee, who was sipping his own hot drink.

"Hello, there, dear boy," he said to me.

"Hi," I offered weakly.

"You had quite an adventure," he said, pushing another hot chocolate my way. This one was topped with whipped cream.

"A failure on every count, I'm afraid," I frowned.

"That's not true," Myrtle said. "I said that I had to give up the jar to save you, but that doesn't mean Draco got it."

I brightened up immediately. "Draco doesn't have it? Tell me the whole story!"

"We are only told our own story," she said, "but I can tell you this much. The sky had started to darken, even though it was midday. I happened to catch a glimpse of Draco in the streets of Jerusalem. This turned out to be you, but I did not know that then. After I confronted you, you fainted. I pulled you and the urn inside the city walls, which were not far away from that spot. We were out of view, but not out of danger. I couldn't carry both of you. I also couldn't leave the pot where Draco might find it, or just dump it out—after all, he may have been watching us. If he was watching us, I knew that if I left you to deal with the pot, he would capture you and ransom you for it.

"I was warned by a Warden that appeared just then that I had good reason to be concerned. It didn't matter; the hairs on my neck had already gone up. I was looking up and down the street through the window of the building, and I was quite certain that a shadowy shape I spied working its way towards us was him. I had to think fast. So, I hid the pot in plain view amongst some other pots that were in the house that I was in, and I carried you out the back. I was going to take you back to first-century Myrtle's abode and face the consequences of having to explain everything... to myself... when there was a fell stench about me. I was surrounded. Just then, a Warden opened a door for me and one of God's holy angels reached in and pulled you through. As for me, I ran as though my life depended on it. It probably did.

"After I thought it was safe to do so, I doubled-back to the place where I had hidden the pot, only to find out that the owner of the place was there, and all the pots were gone. 'I sold them to a member of the Sanhedrin,' he told me. 'Which? For what purpose? What is your business?' I asked. 'I do not know which,' he said, 'but I do know that it was for purposes of burial, for that is what I do—I sell myrrh, aloes, and other spices required for the preparation of the dead.' 'Do you know where I might find this man?' I asked. I was desperate now. 'You see, he purchased every spice I had. Then, he made me swear not to tell, and paid handsomely for my silence. Today, I am made very wealthy. I'm sorry, but I cannot help you.' So, I left."

"It was Joseph of Arimathea or Nicodemus," I said. I remembered that much from my studies.

"If the writer of John can be trusted, it was Nicodemus," Myrtle said. "I did actually know where Nicodemus lived, so I made that my next destination. My time was up, though. While on my way, I was met by messengers, and shortly after that, I was returned to our own. I found that you had been left in my bed; Mr. Chafee stood guard over you until I arrived. Today, after several days of sleeping, you awoke. That is where things are at present."

"So, the blood is safe, then," I said, relieved. "It fell into the hands of one of Jesus' disciples!"

"I have been thinking about it, and I am fairly certain that we did in fact succeed in our quest. The grail fell into the capable hands of Nicodemus or Joseph of Arimathea, or both. For a time, it was out of Draco's reach. I hesitate, though, because just because we kept the pot away from Draco, it doesn't mean he didn't continue on his way to the place of the skull, where there certainly would have been even more blood he could have acquired. Still, it was dark, and the cross was by then surrounded by Roman guards. Plus, the way things worked out, what with the jar falling into the hands of strong protectors, and then the prompt manner in which I was sent back into our present time, I feel like there is a good chance that he did not succeed," she said.

"You do not seem very confident," I observed.

"Well, of course you know that history records numerous rumors of the existence of something called 'the holy grail.' In these rumors, it is usually the cup that Jesus used in his last meal that is referenced, or perhaps a cup used to catch some of Jesus' blood at the cross or shortly before his burial. It goes without saying that these stories caught my husband's attention. Certainly, I also knew that he would be interested. So, many hundreds of years ago, when I first heard these same rumors, I also investigated the matter," Myrtle explained.

"And you learned that there was nothing to those stories?" I asked.

"Ah, well, not exactly. You should know by now that just because stories may change over the years, it doesn't mean there isn't a bit of truth at the core. There was one thing that the stories all had in common..."

She was waiting for me to fill in the blank, but I didn't know what she was getting at.

Mr. Chaffee interjected, "Joseph of Arimathea."

"That's right," Myrtle said. Of course, Mr. Chaffee was a longtime co-conspirator with Myrtle, so he wasn't guessing. He already knew.

Myrtle continued, "Naturally, my husband also would have made this connection. He failed to find the grail for the same reason that I failed to find it: neither of us knew we were looking for a large, ordinary earthen jar filled with ordinary looking dirt."

"But now..." I began. The implications were starting to come clear.

"But now that I have been privileged to see just what the holy grail is, I know that it is very possible that it still exists," Myrtle said. "Unfortunately, by that same privilege, that knowledge is loose in our present day. Granted, the only three humans that have that knowledge are the three that are in this room. Nonetheless, it is knowledge we have that our enemies could extract from us, even if they were trying instead to learn something else. We must guard this knowledge with our lives."

"I swear I will," I said.

"But we must do that while doing something else," Myrtle said.

"What's that?" I asked.

"We must *find* the holy grail."

"So, let me get this straight," I laughed. "Not only am I to help you find and destroy the Tree of Life and the Tree of Knowledge of Good and Evil, I am also to help you find the holy grail?"

"Dear Casey," Myrtle chided me, "remember, you committed to aid me in the battle against *all* of my husband's schemes. They are, I am afraid, numerous and diverse."

"Alright. It just seems like this is getting out of control. I mean, what legend will I discover next is actually true and is my job to deal with?" I asked.

Myrtle winked at me, "Time will tell, my boy. Time will tell."

"So, what next?"

"Obviously, one of our challenges will be looking for the grail without arousing attention or suspicion. If, or shall I say, *when*, my husband learns of our efforts, he will wonder why I have once again turned my eyes to this matter. He will guess that I have acquired new information and will attempt to learn for himself what we know. We must protect ourselves," she said.

"How will we do that?" I inquired.

"You will learn very soon just how many of my children have committed themselves to this fight. Some of these are men and women not to be trifled with. They will protect us. Some of the others are like you in many ways. They are gifted with intuition and the ability to research and analyze and synthesize lots of information, and draw the right conclusions, and contemplate the most proper response. It is time for you to meet them," Myrtle explained.

"People... like me? My brothers and sisters?" I asked, confused.

"More like cousins. And, yes, they are like you, but only so far. They have never caught hold of a Warden and learned their ways. *They* have never visited a past present, let alone seen the very day of Jesus' crucifixion. And they must never learn that *you* have," she said sternly.

I felt chastened, even though I hadn't yet done anything.

"I will keep it strictly to myself," I pledged.

She smiled at me and said, "I know you will try your best."

I smiled back. Really, you can't help but return Myrtle's smile.

"When do we begin?" I asked.

"Immediately, of course!" she said. "I would say, 'pack your things' but you have no 'things' and everything else has been handled for you. I, on the other hand, have a few items I must get in order. Enjoy today on the estate. Tomorrow, bright and early, we depart."

I nodded, and she and Mr. Chaffee excused themselves.

I munched on some of the pastries and fruit that had been left on the table and then went outside. It was a beautiful morning, and Myrtle's property was beautifully manicured. I walked the gardens leisurely. I finally sat down on a bench next to a sparkling pond that mirrored the sky exactly. It was a place of deep tranquility, and delicious scent.

I fell to thinking about my life and the direction it had turned, and the direction it was going.

There had already been adventures, and even more were in the making. Finding the trees, I knew, would take me to the most secluded corners of the globe, for only in such places could such trees grow without being noticed already by mankind. If it still existed, the grail, I reasoned, would probably be in some dark cellar in a historic part of France or England or Europe. My travels were going to be exquisite, to say the least.

"It would be amazing to actually find the grail," I said aloud. "People have been looking for it for more than a thousand years, I bet. To be the one who actually finds it? Awesome."

I closed my eyes and tried to remember the details of what

the jar looked like.

Then, I started thinking about what we would actually do with the grail if we found it. I opened my eyes at the delightful thought, and let my eyes focus on my reflection in the pond. I made eye contact with myself.

"Just think what kind of good we could do if we had the very blood of Jesus in our possession," I said to my reflection.

"Yes, just *think*," it answered back.